TWICE IN
A LIFETIME

Visit us at www.boldstrokesbooks.com

By the Author

TWICE IN A LIFETIME

by

PJ Trebelhorn

2018

TWICE IN A LIFETIME

ISBN 13: 978-1-63555-033-7

THIS TRADE PAPERBACK ORIGINAL IS PUBLISHED BY
BOLD STROKES BOOKS, INC.
P.O. BOX 249
VALLEY FALLS, NY 12185

FIRST EDITION: FEBRUARY 2018

CREDITS
EDITOR: CINDY CRESAP
PRODUCTION DESIGN: SUSAN RAMUNDO
COVER DESIGN BY TAMMY SEIDICK

Acknowledgments

A huge thank you to everyone at Bold Strokes Books, especially Len Barot and Sandy Lowe. I've said it before, but this is an awesome family I feel honored to be a part of.

To my editor, Cindy Cresap, what can I say? You make me a better writer, and you make editing (almost) enjoyable. You're the best.

None of this would be possible without you, the readers, so I thank you all as well. I truly enjoy every email, and Facebook comment I get.

Dedication

For Cheryl, always

Chapter One

Callie Burke jerked her head up and reached for the gun in her shoulder holster. The laughter coming from the passenger side of the car reminded her where she was and what she was doing. Or at least what she was *supposed* to be doing. Sleeping was definitely not it. She scrubbed her face with her hands and sat up straighter in the driver's seat, gripping the steering wheel tightly to keep from strangling the man in the seat next to her.

"You're an ass, Chambers," she said as she stretched her neck and sighed at the satisfying pop it produced. "Have I told you that lately?"

"Pretty sure you find a way to tell me every day, but I know you love me anyway, Burke," her partner, Harry Chambers, replied, still laughing. He was a lifelong cop with the Rochester Police Department, and at almost sixty years old, he was just about twenty years older than Callie, who had celebrated her thirty-ninth birthday a few weeks earlier.

"Yeah, I do, but it doesn't change the fact you're an ass," Callie said, unable to stop the smile his laughter produced. As far as partners went, she could have done a hell of a lot worse. She knew she had Amanda Rodgers, her lieutenant, to thank for pairing them together. Harry didn't have a problem with women on the police force like some of the other male detectives in homicide. "You're lucky I didn't shoot you."

"No, I'm pretty sure you're the one who's lucky you didn't shoot me. The department kind of frowns on things like that, you know?"

"How long was I asleep?"

"Just a couple of minutes." He reached into the backseat and produced a thermos of the best coffee Callie had ever tasted. She quickly grabbed her cup and held it out for a refill, which caused another bout of laughter from him. "And I can pretty much guarantee Deb would never make coffee for you again if you shot me."

"Then you're lucky I like her coffee so much. Just fill my cup, old man," Callie tried to stifle a yawn but was unsuccessful. She glanced at the clock on the dashboard and a feeling of relief washed over her. Their shift was almost over, and Callie couldn't have been happier. She hated spending so much time on stakeouts, especially when the perp they were after hadn't been seen anywhere in the area for well over twenty-four hours. She took a sip of the coffee and closed her eyes with a satisfied groan. "Remind me to kiss Deb the next time I see her."

"Not sure that's going to happen." He chuckled and shook his head.

Yes, Callie owed a debt of gratitude to Amanda for partnering her with Harry. Not only was he respectful of women, but he could have taken offense to what she'd just said. In fact, many of the other guys on the squad would probably have given her a rash of shit for making a suggestive comment about one of their wives.

"I can't wait to get out of here and home to bed. I'm beat," he said with a yawn of his own. "Who knew sitting in a car all night could zap your energy? You going dancing tonight?"

"No, not tonight." Callie had no desire, or energy, to dance tonight, but she could sure as hell use a beer or two. Her sister Quinn was the head bartender at a bar in town and working tonight. Maybe she'd stop in and see her for a few minutes. The bar was within walking distance from her apartment, so if she ended up drinking too much she wouldn't have to worry about how she'd be getting home.

Callie watched in the rearview mirror as another car pulled in behind them. The driver flashed their headlights once before cutting the engine.

"I'll go fill them in," Harry said, reaching for the handle.

Callie closed her eyes and tilted her head back against the headrest. She should probably just go home and sleep, but she hadn't seen Quinn in a few days. She had to stop and think about what day it actually was, because when you were doing stakeouts, the days had a tendency to all run together. She was pretty sure it was Thursday, which meant it had been four days since Sunday brunch with Mom, and the last time she'd seen Quinn.

"All set," Harry said as he got back in the car and rubbed his hands together in an attempt to warm them. "It's going to be another rough winter, I think. It's too freaking cold out there, even for mid-November."

"Shut your mouth, Harry, or you'll make me want to go back to Atlanta." Callie checked her mirrors before pulling out into traffic and heading back to the station. She was kidding because other than the warmer winters in the south, there really wasn't much she'd liked about being there. Especially considering the reasons she'd come back home.

No, she didn't miss Atlanta at all.

❖

Callie took a deep breath before opening the door and walking into the bar. It wasn't a big place, but during the school year it was usually pretty busy with college students. The bar was to the left, a few tables were scattered around a small dance floor, and a separate room in the back had pool tables and dart boards for the people not interested in dancing.

Callie perused the area and noted the high number of women dancing with women, and men dancing with men. Despite the owner and the head bartender both being lesbians, the place had never been advertised as a gay or lesbian bar. The clientele had made it that way. Her eyes stopped on Taylor Fletcher, the owner of the establishment, who was behind the bar talking to Quinn. Callie shook her head and allowed a small smile at the way her heart sped up at the sight of Taylor.

She noticed a couple vacating their stools at the bar, and quickly made her way over to snag one of the seats before anyone else could even think about freezing her out.

She watched silently while Quinn and Taylor finished up whatever business they were discussing, and then Taylor glanced at her and looked like she was about to say something, but then simply shook her head and went back to her office. Callie sighed in defeat.

Taylor had caught her eye not long after her sister started working there, about fifteen years earlier. She had dark brown hair that looked better when it was cut short, as it was now. And although Callie never considered brown eyes attractive, Taylor's were such a pale shade it was nearly impossible to not notice them.

Quinn set a pint in front of her without asking what she wanted. Callie knew her quick look at the rest of the people seated at the bar was all Quinn needed to know she had a few minutes to talk before anyone needed a refill.

"What's up?" she asked Callie.

"Just needed a beer."

"Rough day?"

"Incredibly boring day." Callie chuckled and leaned back in her seat. "I hate stakeouts."

"All the more reason you should come with us for Thanksgiving."

"I can't, Quinn," she said for what felt like the twentieth time. "I've only been back with the Rochester PD for a few months, and there's no way I could ask for a week off so soon."

What she wasn't going to admit to Quinn, or anyone else for that matter, was she would feel uncomfortable at their sister Meg's house. After so many years of not even speaking to Meg and their oldest sister, Beth, it was just too weird to think about visiting for the first time. She was happy they were getting closer, at least to Meg, and Callie even spoke with her on the phone every few days, but talking on the phone and being at her house for a week were worlds apart in her opinion.

"Quinn, you have customers," Taylor said as she walked up beside her.

"Be right back," Quinn said to Callie before heading to the other end of the bar.

Callie was about to say something to Taylor, but she walked away quickly. Yes, she'd always been attracted to Taylor, but she and Andrea, one of Callie's closest friends, had been married, so she never even thought about acting on the attraction. When Andrea, a firefighter, had been killed on the job over three years ago, Taylor never wanted to talk to anyone but Quinn about it, so Callie had kept her distance, which meant she hardly ever came into the bar anymore. She always knew Taylor didn't like her anyway, so staying away wasn't too difficult. She took a sip of her beer and then Quinn was back.

"Don't know what her problem is tonight," Quinn said, looking in the direction Taylor had gone.

"I'm her problem tonight," Callie said without meaning to speak out loud. But since she had, and Quinn's expression gave away her confusion, she went on. "For some reason, the woman hates me."

"Bullshit. Taylor doesn't hate anyone."

"Whatever."

"Why do you think she does?" Quinn leaned forward with her elbows on the bar.

"I *know* she does, Quinn. Andrea told me as much."

"I don't believe it." Quinn shook her head and straightened to wipe the bar down with a towel. "I know Taylor, and she isn't capable of hate."

"She thought I was a bad influence on Andrea." Callie held her glass with both hands and stared into the beer as she spoke. "She thought I was reckless and worried my carelessness would somehow rub off on Andrea. I wouldn't be surprised if she blamed me for Andrea's death."

"You're crazy."

Callie had a feeling there was more to it than what she'd stated to Quinn. Taylor didn't like her because she represented everything Andrea had given up to be with her. Andrea made a commitment, and Callie was still out there, a different woman every night, and Taylor had been worried Andrea would start to miss her old life. At least that was her take on the situation.

But Callie had known Andrea was perfectly happy to give up the life she'd been living. She was so in love with Taylor it made Callie envious. She wanted what they had together, and she thought she'd found it with Jan, who she followed to Atlanta a few months after Andrea died. What a miserable mistake moving with Jan turned out to be when she'd discovered a couple of years later her girlfriend had fallen in love with someone else. She'd left the same day she found out and came back home, only to discover a reawakening of feelings for Taylor she thought had been buried long ago.

Callie downed what was left in her glass and gave Quinn the money for her drink. She put her coat on and turned to leave, but Quinn reached across the bar and grabbed her wrist.

"I don't believe she hates you, and she talked to me a lot in the weeks and months after Andrea died. If she blamed you for what happened, I'd know it. She's never said a word about you to me at all."

Callie wasn't sure what was worse. Taylor not liking her, or Taylor not even caring enough to say anything about her to Quinn. None of it mattered anyway because they were obviously never going to be friends. If for no other reason, Callie was sure every time Taylor saw her she thought about Andrea.

Chapter Two

Taylor sat in her office after closing, finishing up her work for the day. She was distracted, and she really didn't like being distracted. She was at her best when she was focused solely on what she was doing. What should have taken her fifteen minutes to complete was now going on an hour. She sighed and took her glasses off before rubbing her tired eyes.

She didn't understand the strange attraction she was experiencing toward Callie. It wasn't logical, and quite frankly, it was unacceptable. Not to mention completely out of character for her. But what bothered her the most was it made absolutely no sense. It was Saturday night—no, technically Sunday morning—and she hadn't seen Callie for two days. So why the hell was she popping up in her mind now?

"I'm not sure I even like her, for God's sake," she said to the empty room. She took a deep breath and tried to get back into her work. After a few minutes, her mind began to wander again. "Damn it."

After Andrea died, Taylor knew it would have been reasonable to turn to Callie for a shoulder to cry on, but for some reason, she hadn't. Other than her, Callie was the one person who knew Andrea the best. In fact, she was sure Callie knew things about Andrea even she didn't know, and she'd been her wife. Callie had to have been hurting after the loss as well, but in the beginning, Taylor found it easier to place the blame for Andrea's death on Callie. It was wrong to do, and deep down she knew it wasn't anybody's fault. Andrea had run back into the burning building to rescue a child, but she never made it back out. Three other firefighters had died in the same fire. It had been a bad day for the Brockport Fire Department.

"At least I can think about it without choking up now." She wondered briefly when *that* had happened. And the talking to herself. She'd never made a habit of it before. She stood, knowing full well she wasn't going to be able to finish her work tonight, so she grabbed her coat and turned out the lights. She'd just have to come in early tomorrow and finish it.

The drive home took her just about ten minutes, and she smiled when Blaze, her five-year-old golden retriever, met her with his usual puppy-like enthusiasm. The day Andrea brought him home, Taylor fell head over heels in love with him. And every day since then, she loved him even more. They'd leaned on each other after Andrea died, and Taylor was convinced he was just as upset as she'd been when Andrea never came home again.

After she took off her coat and shoes, she led him into the living room and got on the floor with him for their nightly wrestling match. For Blaze, it was more of a love-fest though. Taylor hardly touched him and he flopped over, exposing his belly for a rub.

"You're such a good boy, aren't you?" she said as he wiggled around on his back looking up at her and smiling. She knew he wasn't really smiling, but it certainly looked like he was. He stopped moving and his tail began to thump against the floor.

While he went into the backyard to take care of his business, Taylor washed the few dishes she'd left in the sink before leaving for work earlier. Once Blaze was back inside, she went to the bedroom with him close behind. As usual, he waited patiently for her to get into the bed and get comfortable before jumping up and stretching out beside her, pressed back to back. Taylor glanced at the picture on her bedside table and smiled sadly.

The photo had been taken on their wedding day, and had always been Andrea's favorite of them together. They were laughing at something the photographer had said and looked like they hadn't a care in the world. Taylor sighed as she rolled onto her back, and Blaze rested his chin on her stomach with a whimper. It was almost as though he knew she was sad, and he was trying to tell her it would be all right.

And for the first time in over three years, Taylor was starting to think it just might.

It was sickening, really. Quinn and her girlfriend, Grace, were still in the "can't keep their hands off each other" phase. Callie rolled her eyes from the other side of the table as Grace fed Quinn a piece of bacon with her fingers.

"Get a room," Callie said before shoving a forkful of scrambled eggs in her own mouth.

"Jealous much?" Quinn asked with a smirk.

"Please." Callie shook her head and leaned back in her chair.

"Admit it. You've been jealous of me since the day you were born."

"Both of you knock it off," their mother said. Her tone belied the affection evident in her eyes and the slight smile she gave them.

"We're just teasing each other," Quinn said.

"Well, stop unless you want to send me back to the hospital," she told them.

Callie and Quinn shared a worried glance before Callie turned to their mother.

"Are you feeling all right?" She never wanted to go through that again. Callie was the one who'd found their mother on the floor the day she'd had her heart attack earlier in the year. The feeling of helplessness had been overwhelming, and it had been one of the few times in Callie's life she'd actually been overcome by so much emotion she cried.

"I'm fine," her mother responded with a smirk of her own. "I was just teasing."

"Christ," Callie and Quinn said in unison.

"I swear, sometimes I think you two are still children the way you pick at each other," her mother said as she finally took a seat at the table with them and began putting food on her plate.

"Come on, Linda, if they didn't pick at each other, how would they know they love each other?" Grace asked. When Callie glanced at her, Grace batted her eyelashes and gave her an innocent smile.

"When are you guys leaving for Philly?" Callie asked, looking down at her plate to hide her grin. Grace knew them so well it was unnerving at times.

"Trying to get rid of us?" Quinn asked.

"Absolutely." Callie nodded and stood to get herself another cup of coffee. "I have big plans for a party at your house, so I need to know when I can tell everyone to show up."

"We're leaving Tuesday morning, and we'll be back on Sunday," Grace said without even looking at her.

Callie could tell they all knew she was only joking, which almost made her want to really throw a party. Almost. If there was one thing she hated, it was being predictable.

"Cool. Friday night it is," she said before topping off everyone's coffee.

"If there is anything out of place when we get back, you're never house-sitting for us again," Quinn said. Callie smiled and took her seat again after returning the coffee pot to the counter.

"Why do you need a house sitter, anyway?" Callie asked. "You don't have any pets, and you have no plants. Which, I should point out, if you did have plants, they wouldn't still be alive by the time you got back."

"Because it makes me feel important to tell people I have a house sitter." Quinn shrugged. "And I thought you might want to stay somewhere other than the one-room apartment you live in above Grace's book store."

"Hey, now, I lived there for years and you never seemed to care then," Grace said.

"Why don't you come with us?" her mother asked as she placed a hand on Callie's forearm. Callie was just grateful she'd changed the subject when she did. The only thing worse than Quinn and Grace all lovey-dovey was Quinn and Grace arguing. It didn't happen often, but when it did, it made Callie uncomfortable. "I really don't like the idea of you spending Thanksgiving all alone."

"I won't be alone, Mom." Callie sighed. It wasn't a lie, because she'd no doubt be working on Thanksgiving. Unless something broke in the case and they managed to locate their suspect, which at this point seemed highly unlikely.

"Hot date?" Grace asked with a grin and a wink.

"I'm not sure Harry Chambers would ever be accused of being a *hot date*." Callie chuckled. Now she was going to lie, but she figured it was small enough to not hurt anyone, and besides, it would make her mother feel better about going without her. "He and his wife invited me for Thanksgiving dinner."

"Really?" her mother asked, her tone indicating she didn't believe her. "That's awfully nice of them."

"They're good people." Callie took a sip of her coffee. "Although I don't know what I'll do next Sunday without all this food."

Sunday brunch was a tradition their mother started when Quinn had moved out on her own. Their mother had been afraid she'd never see Quinn again, so it was a way to guarantee she'd come visit once a week. Once started, the ritual never stopped, and Callie secretly looked forward to it every week.

CHAPTER THREE

Callie looked at the clock on the dashboard and sighed loudly. Seven thirty, which meant they still had over three hours until the end of their shift, and she was fighting to stay awake. She glanced at Harry and saw he was struggling as well.

"Deb didn't send nearly enough coffee with you tonight," Callie remarked.

"It's the biggest thermos we have," he said. "Can't send more than there's room for."

"Maybe I'll get you one of those huge ones for Christmas."

"Jesus, we'd better not still be out here doing this in another month."

They both watched the building again for a few minutes, but then Callie felt her eyes growing heavy again.

"Time for dinner?" she asked. There was a hamburger joint a couple of blocks away, and it was Harry's turn to make the walk to get their food. Thank God for that. It was too cold to have to go out there.

"The usual?" he asked as he reached for the door handle.

"I'm feeling adventurous tonight," she said with a grin. "Get it with onions this time."

He chuckled as he got out, but he leaned down and looked at her before closing the door. "If he comes out of there, you call for backup and wait here. No heroics, Burke, understood?"

"Yeah, yeah" she said absently as she redirected her gaze to the building their suspect was currently living in. At least they thought he was still living there. No one had seen him at all in almost a week. He was probably on the other side of the country by now. "Understood."

She watched Harry until he turned the corner then grabbed the thermos that held what little remained of Deb's heavenly coffee and poured it into her travel mug. Just as she took her first sip, she saw the front door of the apartment building open, and their suspect stuck his head out to look up and down the street.

"Holy shit," she muttered as she fumbled for her police radio. She called it in and slouched down in her seat as she watched him heading in the opposite direction of where Harry had gone. Wasn't this just typical. There alone, and backup was five minutes away. And the asshole picks now to show his face. When he disappeared into an alley, Callie had to make a decision. Did she sit there and wait for backup, or did she go after him on foot—and alone?

Without dwelling on it too long, she pulled her service weapon out and opened the door. If she had anything to say about it, this was the last night they'd have to sit out here in the car for their entire shift. She tried to be quiet as she kept against the wall of the building and made her way slowly down the alley.

It was dark, and the only light came from the streetlamps behind her and the streetlamps at the other end of the alley. A noise a few feet ahead of her made her stop and hold her breath, her heart racing as her eyes strained to adjust to the darkness.

Maybe going after him on her own wasn't the smartest idea she'd ever had, but it was too late to turn back now.

"Stop! Police!"

A feeling of relief washed over her momentarily at the voice coming from the opposite end of the alley, until she realized there was someone running right toward her. She stepped away from the wall and aimed her gun low so she could hit him in the leg, as well as to not do any significant damage to the officers chasing him back toward her if she were to miss.

"Shit!" she heard, right before she felt the searing pain in her right shoulder that came in near unison of the sound of their suspect firing his gun.

Callie dropped her gun and fell to her knees before she heard Harry and a couple other voices yelling, and then everything went black.

❖

"This day is never going to end," Taylor said to Camille, her head bartender in Quinn's absence. "I can't believe it's only nine o'clock."

"Tell me about it," Camille responded. "And there's almost no business on top of it."

"If it stays like this, I'll probably let you go home early."

Taylor headed back to her office, but before she got there, she felt her phone vibrating in her back pocket. She pulled it out and grinned when she saw it was Quinn. The woman couldn't even take a vacation.

"You do know you don't need to check up on me, right?" she said by way of answering the call.

"Taylor, thank God," Quinn said, sounding frantic.

"What's wrong? Are you okay? Grace? Your mother?"

"What? No, we're all fine, but I got a call from Strong Memorial."

"What happened?"

"Callie's been shot."

Taylor heard a slight hitch in Quinn's voice, and felt her own breath catch in her throat. She knew how close Quinn and Callie were, and she couldn't imagine how Quinn might handle it if something were to be seriously wrong with her younger sister.

"Is she okay?" Taylor somehow managed around the lump in her throat. Despite her best efforts, her mind flashed back to the day Andrea died. The tone of the call then had been much different though. She shook her head. This wasn't the same thing. Callie had to be all right. For Quinn.

"The doctor said she should make a full recovery, but I'm not convinced she didn't persuade him to assure me of that," Quinn said with a nervous laugh. "I was hoping I could talk you into going over there and checking on her for me."

"Of course." Taylor grabbed her coat and somehow managed to get it on without taking the phone from her ear. "I'll head there now and call as soon as I know something."

"Thanks, Taylor. You're the best."

Taylor ended the call and hurried out to the bar. She was suddenly glad it was a slow night as she tapped Camille on the shoulder.

"I'm afraid I won't be able to let you go early tonight." Taylor quickly checked to make sure she had her keys and her wallet before buttoning up her coat. "Quinn just called from Philadelphia, and Callie's been shot. I need to run to the hospital to make sure she's okay."

"No problem. Go, I've got this."

Taylor was halfway to the hospital before she allowed herself to think about Andrea again. It had been months since she'd reflected on the day her life had changed forever, mostly because she knew dwelling on it wouldn't bring her back, and damn it, it was downright depressing.

She'd rushed to the hospital then too, but the difference back then was she'd already known Andrea wasn't going to make it. She was going there to say good-bye, but Andrea hadn't even known she was there. Andrea's chief had called to tell Taylor the extent of her injuries and to let her know she was in grave condition and unresponsive upon arriving at the hospital. They managed to keep her alive long enough for her to get there, and Taylor seriously thought she was going to die that day too because her heart had hurt so much.

She shook her head and roughly brushed away the tears. This was totally different, she reminded herself again. She wasn't going to walk into the hospital and find Andrea lying on a gurney, clinging to the final moments of her life. It was more likely she'd walk in and find Callie flirting with any attractive female in the vicinity. At least she hoped she would for Quinn's sake. Taylor had no siblings, so she had no idea of the bond the two of them shared.

Quinn had apparently told the staff she was going to be coming by, because when she told the woman at the desk who she was there for, she was immediately taken to Callie's room. The sight of Callie, motionless and pale, stopped her in her tracks.

"The doctor should be in shortly," the nurse said quietly as she left her there alone.

There was a man asleep in a chair next to Callie's bed, and Taylor wondered who he was. He was older, and she briefly wondered if it could be Callie and Quinn's father. She dismissed the thought almost as quickly as it surfaced though because Quinn told her their father had left when she was just seven, and they'd never seen or heard from him again.

As she made her way quietly into the room, she noticed the badge on his belt, and it dawned on her he must be Callie's partner. She cleared her throat in an attempt to wake him without being obvious about it.

His eyes popped open and he sat up straighter as he watched her warily. She figured it must be a trait inherent in police officers. He stood and gave what seemed to Taylor to be a forced smile as he extended his hand.

"Harry Chambers," he said, his voice strained, whether from sleep or emotion she couldn't say. "I'm Callie's partner."

"Were you there when it happened?" Taylor shook his hand briefly before turning to look at Callie again. She seemed so helpless.

"I'm sorry, but who are you?"

"Oh, I apologize," she said, her cheeks heating with embarrassment because her parents raised her better. "Taylor Fletcher. Callie's sister, Quinn, works for me. She's in Philadelphia for the holiday and asked if I would come check on Callie for her."

"I see," he said, seeming to finally relax. He went to the edge of Callie's bed and looked down at her with what appeared to be genuine affection. "She went after a suspect in an alley. Uniformed officers came in from the other end, and the guy was trapped. Since there were two of them, and Callie was alone, I guess he figured his chances were better against her."

"Why was she alone? Weren't you with her?"

"I'd gone to get dinner for us." Harry shook his head slightly, and when he glanced at her, she saw a tear rolling down his cheek. It was clear this guy cared very much for Callie. "I told her to wait for backup if he happened to show himself, but she must have thought he was going to get away."

"Reckless," Taylor murmured. Just like Andrea told her. She'd always said Callie would chase after the devil himself if she thought she had a chance in hell of catching him.

"I wouldn't say that," Harry said, shaking his head. "Don't get me wrong. I'm pissed as hell at her for not waiting, but I can certainly understand why she did it. Surveillance is a boring job. We'd been out there for over a week and never set eyes on him once. She saw the opportunity to end it and went after him. You should know she did radio dispatch to send other officers first though."

"Damn right, I did," Callie muttered just before her eyes fluttered open. She glanced around the room, stopping when her eyes met Taylor's. *What the hell is she doing here?* She closed her eyes again, mostly because the overhead light was way too bright. "I did exactly what you would have done, Chambers."

"Yeah, you did," he said as he grasped her hand. "I have to go call Deb and let her know you're awake."

Callie lay there with her eyes still closed until she heard the door shut, then opened them again to see Taylor watching her. She looked like she was seriously irritated.

"Are you going to be all right?" she asked quietly. "What did the doctors say?"

"Don't know," Callie said with an attempted shrug, but she winced at the fire shooting through her right shoulder at the movement. "I just joined this party myself."

That was when she noticed her right shoulder was bandaged, and her arm was immobilized against her body. She gently lifted the hospital gown with her left hand and saw some blood seeping through the bandage. There wasn't much, but it brought back what had happened with amazing clarity. She'd been shot. God damn, it hurt.

"Good to see you're awake," a male voice said from the doorway. Callie grinned in spite of her pain at the sight of Dr. David Randall. She'd known him since high school. "How are you feeling, Calliope?"

"You know damn well my name isn't Calliope, David," she said with a slight growl in her voice and a quick glance at Taylor. She didn't want anyone thinking her name was actually Calliope. It wasn't necessarily a bad name, but it just wasn't for her. He'd started calling her that in their junior year, and he continued to do it every time he saw her for no other reason than he knew how much it aggravated her.

"All right, all right, I'll give you a break this time, but only because you've been shot." He threw his hands up in mock surrender before turning his attention to Taylor with a smile. "And who is this?"

"Taylor Fletcher," she answered, looking back and forth between him and Callie.

"David Randall," he said as he took Callie's chart from the end of the bed. He opened it as he asked, "And how long have you two been together?"

"What?" Taylor asked, the surprise evident in her voice. She shook her head a little too aggressively in Callie's opinion. "We aren't together."

"My sister works for her," Callie said quickly.

"Quinn? How is she doing?" he asked. "I spoke to her briefly when I called to tell her you were here, but it didn't seem to be the time for chitchat."

"She's doing great," Callie said as she rested her head back against the pillow. "But I'm more interested in how I'm doing at the moment."

"You'll survive," he said with a grin. He placed the chart back where he'd gotten it and pulled a penlight out of his pocket so he could check her pupils. "The bullet passed through without hitting anything vital. A little more serious than a graze, but not by much. Basically, all I had to do was clean it out and stitch you up."

"When can I go home?"

"Ready to leave so soon?" he asked, placing a hand over his heart as though her words wounded him. He laughed when she just glared at him. "As long as you don't do anything to piss me off between now and then, I don't see any reason why you can't be discharged in the morning."

"Thank God," she said.

"Of course, you'll need someone to stay with you for a few days. You'll have limited mobility in your right arm for a while."

"I live alone, and Quinn's out of town until Sunday," she said, but then she worried Quinn might be rushing back home. She looked at Taylor. "She's not coming home early because of this, is she?"

"I don't think so. She called and asked me to come check on you. I just assumed as long as you were okay, she wasn't going to cut her trip short."

"If you don't have someone to stay with, I can't let you go home." David shook his head and checked her blood pressure.

"She can stay with me." Taylor said, looking about as shocked at having said the words as Callie felt upon hearing them. She pulled her phone out of her pocket and held it up. "I should go call Quinn and let her know you're all right."

"You sure you aren't together?" David asked when she was gone.

"We aren't even friends."

"Uh-huh," he said as he wrote something in her chart. "Maybe you should rethink things, Burke. She's quite the looker."

"Yeah, trust me, I know."

"Does she play for your team?"

"Jesus, do you know how juvenile you sound? Yes, she's a lesbian, so don't even think about it."

"I won't, and my wife would have my head if I did." He smiled as he walked backward toward the door. "But I think you should give it a lot of thought, if you know what I mean."

He was gone before Callie could even think about forming a response. She sighed. She was certain Taylor only saw her as Quinn's little sister. And her late wife's best friend. Oh, yeah, and as a woman Taylor didn't even like. She was already looking forward to Sunday so she could stay with Quinn or her mother. Callie had a feeling it was certainly going to be a long few days until then.

On the other hand, it might give her an opportunity to convince Taylor she wasn't so bad after all. To show her she wasn't a reckless buffoon. Maybe this kind of challenge was exactly what she needed. Maybe it could end up being what they both needed. The thought made her smile.

It was nice to fantasize sometimes, and she hoped she could keep the fantasy going, at least in her mind, until Sunday.

Chapter Four

Taylor stepped outside the front doors of the emergency room and pulled her phone from her pocket. She scrolled through to find Quinn's number, but before placing the call, she looked up at the sky.

"What the hell am I doing? Oh, sure, *she can stay with me*," she muttered a little too loudly for it to be considered under her breath. "God, help me. I just know she's going to drive me insane."

She leaned against the building then and noticed Harry sitting on a bench a few feet to her right, just putting his own phone away.

Jesus Christ, I have got to stop talking to myself.

"Did the doctor ever come in?" To his credit, he didn't say a word about her talking to absolutely no one, but she knew he had to have heard her.

"Yes, he said she can go home in the morning, as long as she doesn't do anything to piss him off."

Harry smiled and shook his head, and Taylor couldn't help but return the smile.

"Good luck with that," he said. "Sometimes I think that kid was put on this earth for no other reason than to piss off people in authority."

The term *kid* surprised Taylor because she knew Callie was close to forty. But she supposed it was possible for Harry to be old enough to be her father, so she admitted the term made a strange kind of sense.

"Don't get me wrong," Harry said, evidently interpreting her expression the wrong way. "She's one of the best people I know. She's got a big heart, and she'd give a stranger the shirt off her back if they needed it. But unfortunately she has a tendency to rub people the wrong way sometimes, if you know what I mean."

"I do, trust me," Taylor answered with a nod. By the look he gave her, she realized she probably agreed with his assessment a little too quickly. What did it matter now though? He was no doubt already convinced she was a nut job.

"Well, I should get back in there." He headed for the doors but stopped and looked at her before going through. "It was nice meeting you, Taylor Fletcher."

"You too." She smiled as she placed the phone to her ear. His praise of Callie seemed to her to be a little naïve. Or maybe he just misinterpreted her connection to Callie. Either way, it left Taylor feeling a bit off-kilter. She was so lost in her thoughts it startled her when she heard Quinn's voice in her ear.

"Is she all right?" Quinn said without preamble.

"She's fine," Taylor said, picturing her sitting there waiting anxiously, the phone gripped tightly in her hand as she waited for her to call. "The doctor said the bullet didn't hit anything vital, and she'll be discharged in the morning."

"Wow," Quinn said with a chuckle. "I thought she'd be there for a few days at least. I guess I was worried for nothing. We can be back tomorrow evening."

"You don't need to come back." Taylor knew she should have taken the out Quinn was offering, but she didn't see any good reason to make them come home before the weekend. "I told the doctor she could stay with me for a few days."

"Are you sure?" Quinn sounded skeptical, but Taylor chose to ignore it. "I mean, she isn't your responsibility. What about the bar?"

"I'm sure Camille can handle things for the most part, and Callie can manage to take care of herself if I need to go in for a few hours, don't you think?"

"Weren't you going to your parents' house for dinner on Thursday?"

"It's not a big deal, Quinn. Just enjoy the holiday and I'm certain I'll be more than ready for you to take her off my hands when you get back on Sunday."

"Are you sure?"

"Good night, Quinn," Taylor said with a grin even though she knew Quinn couldn't see it.

"I owe you one."

"You'll owe me more than one, trust me." They both laughed before saying their good-byes and hanging up.

Taylor looked up at the sky and wondered again what the hell she was thinking when she offered to let Callie stay with her. And why she hadn't simply agreed when Quinn said they'd come home tomorrow.

"Please just let me get through the next few days without killing her," she said under her breath.

"Where the hell have you been hiding that one, Burke?" Harry asked when he came back into her room. He shook his head. "I swear to God, you have all the luck with the ladies. You could leave a few for the rest of us poor schmucks."

"Don't let Deb hear you say that," Callie said with a grin.

"I'm allowed to look," he said defiantly. "She'd kill me if I ever did more than that though. But tell me about this Taylor Fletcher."

"There's nothing to tell," Callie assured him. She pushed the button on her little remote to raise the head of the bed.

"Bullshit," Harry said with a chuckle. "A woman who looks like she does comes to your room mere hours after you've been shot, and there's nothing to tell? Try again."

Callie was quiet for a minute. Harry had met Andrea a couple of times, so maybe he would understand. She decided to take a chance.

"You remember my friend, Andrea? The firefighter?"

"Sure. She was killed in that house fire where three other guys died too, right? About three years ago?"

"Closer to three and a half, but yeah, that was her." Callie nodded. "Taylor was her wife."

"Oh," Harry said quietly. He sat in the chair he'd pulled up next to the bed and looked at her. Callie wondered what it was he might be seeing. "She was your best friend, right? Did you have an affair with her wife?"

"No!" Callie said, a bit too loud. "Jesus, Harry, I would never do that."

"I didn't think so, but I had to ask. You like her though, right? Is she single?"

"It doesn't matter."

"The hell it doesn't, Burke," he said. "You didn't see her when she first walked in here. The way she looked at you. She was seriously worried about you."

"More likely she was thinking about Andrea being in the hospital the day she died." Callie hoped she was wrong and Harry was right, but she had the feeling it was exactly as she said. Taylor had looked irritated to be there. Annoyed. Callie was sure the only reason she was there at all was because Quinn had been out of town.

"Oh well, she's crazy anyway," Harry said with a laugh.

Callie shook her head at his change in direction. It was just how Harry was. He knew she was right, so now he was telling her why she was lucky to not be with Taylor. When she'd first met him, this odd character trait of his had made her head hurt, but she'd grown to accept it over the years. She just wished she hadn't zoned out and taken off to Atlanta for almost two years.

"Okay, I'll bite," Callie said. "Why is she crazy?"

"She was standing outside talking to herself."

"Like you don't do it yourself about thirty times in an eight-hour shift."

"Yeah, but you already know I'm crazy," he said with a grin. "You should be happy I found this out about her before you worked up the nerve to make a move."

She laughed with him, but then the thought dawned on her—she didn't really know what had happened to her. Not everything, anyway. Clearly, she'd been shot, but she didn't remember much from the time Harry got out of the car to get their dinner until she'd woken up in this bed.

"Did we get him?" she asked.

"I'm sorry?"

"Alton? Our murder suspect? Don't tell me I took a bullet for nothing, Chambers."

"Yeah, we got him." Harry chuckled. "He tripped over your big ass feet and fell flat on his face. He's in an interrogation room downtown with Rodgers."

"Amanda's questioning him herself?" Callie was surprised. Interrogating suspects was usually the detective's job.

"She never completely got away from her days in our shoes," Harry said. "And if Alton knows what's good for him, he'll cooperate with her."

"Damn straight on that one," she laughed. Lieutenant Amanda Rodgers had mastered the good cop, bad cop routine. Many suspects over the years had tried to stonewall her questioning, but she almost always got them to break eventually.

Callie hoped someday she could be half as good at her job as Amanda was at hers.

CHAPTER FIVE

"Hi, Mom," Taylor said when she answered the phone the next morning. She was just getting ready to walk out the door to pick Callie up from the hospital. She'd called them the night before to let them know she wouldn't be able to come for dinner the next day, and they'd sounded more disappointed than she'd expected them to be.

"Honey, your father and I talked about it, and we decided we'll be coming to you for Thanksgiving this year," her mother said, sounding like the matter was settled. Which, of course, it was. Eleanor Fletcher always had the last word.

"What?" Taylor panicked as she looked around her kitchen. She had no food in the house. At least nothing to qualify for a holiday dinner. Unless of course they wanted to settle for frozen pizza, or maybe peanut butter and jelly sandwiches. She glanced into the refrigerator. Nope, no jelly, so sandwiches were out. "I am so not prepared to make dinner."

"Aren't you sweet?" her mother asked, sounding amused. "We know you don't cook, dear. I'm going to cook everything here today, and we'll just heat it up tomorrow when we get to your house."

"I don't know, Mom," she said. She wasn't sure she wanted Callie to meet her parents. Or, more accurately, she wasn't sure she wanted her parents to meet Callie. She knew they would jump to the wrong conclusion. They'd been pestering her for the past year to start dating again, and although Taylor thought she was getting close to being able to do it, she wasn't quite there yet. Not to mention the fact Callie would definitely *not* be her first choice. Or even her second. Or third. No, Callie wouldn't be anywhere on her list of women to date. Of course, no such list existed, so...

"Come on, honey, it's Thanksgiving."

"Don't disappoint your mother, Taylor," her father said.

"Really, Dad? Why don't you people get cell phones like everyone else in the world?" Taylor pretended to be irritated, but the teasing was evident in her tone. Both of her parents laughed.

"And miss out on being able to listen in from the other room?" her dad asked. "Pretty sure that won't be happening any time soon, dear."

"Whatever," Taylor said, finally giving in, just as they all knew she would eventually. "What time will you be here?"

"Around noon," her mother said. "That way we can eat at one."

"Okay, I'll see you tomorrow." Taylor started to disconnect the call, but she heard her father say something. "What, Dad?"

"I said we're looking forward to meeting your friend."

"She's not a friend. I told you that last night."

After they hung up, she hesitated for a moment. If Callie wasn't at least a friend, then why was Taylor letting her stay with her? Because she's Quinn's sister, she thought. And because she'd been one of Andrea's best friends. The strange attraction she felt to her had absolutely nothing to do with it.

Nothing at all.

❖

Callie smiled at Taylor when she walked into the room, but she was still listening to the instructions David was giving her. Don't get it wet, don't overdo things, blah, blah, blah. She was listening, but she surely wasn't hearing any of it.

"You might want to tell her," Callie said, indicating Taylor, who was standing behind him. "You have me on such awesome painkillers, I'm never going to remember a damn thing you're telling me."

He laughed and shook his head before turning to Taylor and going through it all again. Callie watched Taylor, who was apparently listening very intently to what he was saying.

A nurse had helped her to get dressed earlier, so Callie was all ready to go. She wanted to be out of this place. Hospitals freaked her out, although there was no reason why they should. Her arm was in a sling that was attached to her torso so she couldn't move it. Trying to do everything with her left hand could possibly be her demise.

David and Taylor were finally finished with their conversation, and Callie got to her feet.

"Let's get out of here," Callie said.

"Not quite yet," David said. "A nurse will be in with your discharge papers." He looked at Taylor. "Make sure she doesn't do anything she shouldn't. Her shoulder needs to heal, and I know her well enough to predict she'll try and push her boundaries. Don't let her."

"I won't," Taylor said, shooting a glance at Callie that told her in no uncertain terms she meant business. Once David was gone Callie sat once more, hoping she'd never have to be on the receiving end of such a look again.

"He's no fun."

"Callie, you were shot. I really don't think this is meant to be fun."

"If you believe I think any of this is fun, then you don't know me very well." Callie fought to keep her voice down because she really didn't feel up to arguing with Taylor.

"No, I don't know you. How could I? You never came to the house."

"Only because Andrea told me you didn't like me." Callie sighed as she raked her fingers through her hair. "I never came to the house because I didn't want to cause problems for the two of you."

Taylor stared at her, and Callie refused to look away. Based on Taylor's expression, Callie would have guessed she knew nothing about what Andrea told her. But that was crazy, wasn't it? Why would Andrea have lied to her about it?

"I never told her I didn't like you," Taylor said, her voice quiet. She shook her head. "I swear to you I never said that."

"But it's true, isn't it?"

"We've already established I don't really know you," Taylor said as she took a seat in a chair a few feet away from her. "I can't honestly say one way or the other. You were a good friend to Andrea, something for which I'll always be grateful. What I don't like is this. You getting shot and acting as though it's no big deal. You joke about things you shouldn't."

"I joke about things that make me uncomfortable," Callie said. But why was she telling her? She'd never admitted it to anyone. Not even Andrea. "And believe me, it makes me plenty uncomfortable to realize if he'd shot me on the left side instead of the right, I might be dead. If that makes *you* uncomfortable, then I'm sorry. You don't have to do this. I'm sure I can manage to take care of myself for a few days until Quinn gets back."

"Don't be ridiculous. I said I'd help by taking care of you, and I will. I canceled my trip to have Thanksgiving at my parents' house, so you're not going to make me have done that for no damn reason. Understand?"

Callie tried not to smile, but Taylor being bossy was kind of cute. She only nodded in response because she didn't trust herself to not say something inappropriate. Luckily, the nurse chose that moment to enter the room with the papers she needed to sign. She was also pushing a wheelchair.

"Oh, hell, no. I don't need one of those," Callie said, motioning toward the wheelchair as she handed the papers back to her. "I can walk out of here just fine on my own."

"Humor me," the woman said, but she didn't appear to be very jovial to Callie. "I know cops tend to be a tough group, but it is hospital policy."

"Just get in the damn chair," Taylor said as she stood and gripped the handles.

"Yes, ma'am." Callie got into the chair without any further argument. This was definitely going to be an interesting few days.

❖

"Come in with me?" Callie asked when Taylor pulled her car up to the bookstore she lived above.

"I'll wait here." Taylor shut off the engine and crossed her arms over her chest, an obvious sign she was irritated about all of this.

"Listen, I know you aren't happy about having to help me out, but can we at least try to get along?" Callie asked. God knew she wasn't entirely happy about it either, but Taylor had been the one who offered her assistance. She looked at the door to the staircase leading up to her apartment. "I'm not sure I can navigate the staircase and carry a bag with the use of only one hand."

Taylor didn't respond, but simply got out of the car and went to wait for her at the door to the building. She was pissed, but Callie didn't know why. Was it something about her, or was it because of what she'd said about Andrea?

"I'm sorry, Callie," Callie muttered under her breath as she struggled to get out of the passenger side without the use of her right arm. "Of course I'll help you."

"Did you say something?" Taylor asked.

"Nope, not a word." She slammed the car door and plastered a smile on her face.

They didn't speak as she shoved some clothes into her duffel bag, mostly sweatshirts and sweatpants, because what else could she possibly need? It wasn't like there was a fancy dinner planned anywhere, right? She grabbed a pair of jeans just in case. She went and quickly grabbed things from the bathroom she would need. She sighed and looked at Taylor, who was standing at the window looking at the street below. Callie didn't think she'd actually noticed the apartment when she walked in. She'd simply gone straight to the window and hadn't looked back.

"Could you zip this closed for me, please?"

Taylor came and did it without a word, then carried it to the door. "Do you have everything you need?"

"I hope so," Callie said. She stood there and watched as Taylor walked out the door and down the stairs. "She might be harder to break than I thought."

Chapter Six

Taylor was still fuming when she pulled into her garage. She'd never said anything to Andrea about not liking Callie. Why in the world would she have told Callie she did? It didn't make any sense at all to her. Maybe she'd said something about not liking the fact Callie was so reckless, which wasn't the same as not liking her, was it?

"I'm sorry you're going to have to miss spending Thanksgiving with your parents," Callie said as they walked into the house.

Taylor didn't respond. She was grateful Callie had been quiet not only on the ride to her apartment to get the things she'd need for the few days at Taylor's, but then again on the ride to Taylor's house. She didn't know how to talk to Callie. There was a strange feeling inside her because part of her wanted to be nice to Callie and try to get to know her better, but the other part balked at the idea of letting her in at all. The attraction she was feeling really wasn't helping much either.

Blaze met them at the door, excited as usual to see her, but when he noticed Callie, he sat down and cocked his head to the side, watching her intently. His tail was sweeping slowly back and forth. Tentatively.

"Do you think he remembers me?" Callie asked quietly.

"You've met him?" Her surprise must have been evident by the way Callie looked at her.

"I was with Andrea the day she got him. He was an anniversary gift if I recall correctly."

"Yes," Taylor said, scratching Blaze behind the ear with her free hand. She set Callie's bag down and tried her best to not let Callie see she was close to crying at the memory she invoked. "He was. I doubt he'd remember you though. He was just a puppy at the time."

She watched as Callie held her hand out to him. Blaze leaned forward and sniffed her hand for a moment before shoving his head under it and wagging his tail so furiously his entire body shook. Callie laughed, and Taylor couldn't help but join in.

"I think you might be wrong about that," Callie said.

"I guess so," Taylor said in amazement. Blaze was never this friendly to people he didn't know. He was usually wary and kept his distance until he'd had the chance to figure them out. "It looks like you've got a new friend."

"Just one?" Callie glanced at her. "What do I have to do in order to win you over too?"

Taylor just shook her head as she picked Callie's bag up again and led her down the hall.

"Unfortunately, my guest room isn't set up for guests. It's my exercise room. So you'll have to sleep in my room, and I'll take the couch."

"No." Callie reached out and caught Taylor's wrist. "I won't let you do that. I can sleep on the couch."

"It's not a big deal, really," Taylor said. She looked at Callie's hand, which was still wrapped around her wrist. After another moment, Callie released her and took a step back.

"I've ruined your holiday plans. I won't inconvenience you in your own home too."

"You didn't ruin my holiday plans," Taylor said. "My parents are coming here instead."

"Oh." Callie looked horrified. "Okay, well, I can make myself scarce while they're here."

"What?" Taylor laughed and shook her head. "Not necessary. They know you're here, and there will be more than enough food. You're staying for dinner."

"You know, you're kind of cute when you're bossy."

"Excuse me?" Taylor looked at her, not quite believing what she'd heard. At least Callie had the decency to blush at her comment. She turned away, not wanting Callie to see the grin she couldn't hide.

"I'm sorry. I really do need to learn how to filter what goes from my brain to my mouth."

"This is where you'll sleep," Taylor said, choosing to ignore her remark, but silently agreed with her assessment. "I just need to get a few things out of the bathroom."

"I don't feel good about this," Callie said as she sat on the edge of the bed. "You should be able to sleep in your own bed."

"Trust me, before you deal with my parents, and given the fact they refuse to believe you aren't the new woman in my life, you'll need a good night's sleep." Taylor shut the bathroom door and looked at herself in the mirror. Maybe she needed to learn how to filter as well. She couldn't believe she'd said the words out loud.

Taylor walked into the kitchen after taking a shower later the same afternoon to find Callie going through her cupboards, so she leaned against the doorframe and watched her for a moment. She'd have to be blind to not notice how attractive Callie was. There was nothing wrong with appreciating how good-looking someone was. It didn't have to mean anything, right?

Callie grinned when she looked over her shoulder and caught Taylor checking her out. Taylor refused to look away, even though her cheeks were burning with embarrassment at being discovered.

"Do you like the view?" Callie asked with a cocky grin.

"What view?" Taylor snorted. "In case you've forgotten, you're wearing sweats. You could have been anyone here in my kitchen going through my things."

"Okay, if that's what you want to tell yourself." Callie took a seat at the table but never broke their eye contact. Taylor finally did when it got to be too intense.

"What do you want for dinner?" she asked, making her way to the fridge.

"Based on what I found? Potato chips, ice cream, and cookies." Callie chuckled. "I thought you were cooking Thanksgiving dinner tomorrow. How are you going to make a meal out of the junk food you have?"

"I never said I was cooking," Taylor said defensively without turning around. "I said my parents were coming here for dinner. They're cooking everything and bringing it with them because they know I can't boil water without setting off the smoke alarms."

She expected some sarcastic comeback, but instead was met with silence. She stood up from where she was bent over looking into the refrigerator and looked at Callie, who was watching her from her seat at the table.

"Just for the record?" Callie asked, meeting her eyes. "I like the view."

Taylor felt a blush taking over her cheeks once again as she realized Callie had been staring at her ass while she was bent over. Christ, this was the first day, and already Callie was flirting mercilessly with her. She so wanted to say something she'd no doubt regret, but then remembered Andrea telling her she needed to learn how to take a compliment.

"Thank you," she said before turning away again. She took a deep breath and opened the drawer where she kept the takeout menus. She dropped them on the table and walked out of the kitchen as she tossed over her shoulder, "Figure out what you want and I'll call it in."

She went right to the bathroom and closed the door. She sat on the edge of the tub and leaned over, her head in her hands. This wasn't right. She shouldn't be allowing Callie to flirt with her. Definitely not in the home she'd shared with Andrea. She had to admit though, it felt good to be appreciated by a woman again. Flirting didn't have to lead anywhere, right? Especially with Callie. She reminded herself Callie no doubt flirted with every woman, just like her sister Quinn used to do before she'd finally settled down with Grace.

But even if she didn't flirt with everyone, nothing would ever happen between the two of them. After losing her firefighter wife, there was no way she'd ever get involved with another woman in a high-risk job. Especially after Callie had just been shot. She shook her head.

She could try to convince herself it was true all she wanted, but it did nothing to explain the fluttering she felt in her belly every time Callie smiled at her.

"Want to watch a movie?" Taylor asked while she was putting the leftovers from their dinner in the refrigerator.

Eating hadn't been easy with only the use of her left hand, but Callie figured pizza would have been simple enough. Boy, had she been wrong. No one would ever accuse her of being ambidextrous, as it was painfully obvious she was pretty much useless without her dominant hand.

"I don't know," Callie said, remembering the only place to sit in the living room was the couch. She didn't think she could keep from sitting too close to Taylor. Sure, they'd been flirting back and forth, but there were so many walls up around Taylor, it would likely take a battering ram to knock them down. "I'm pretty tired."

"It's only seven o'clock," Taylor said, sounding unconvinced.

"I was shot last night, remember?"

"Fine." Taylor seemed disappointed, and the last thing Callie wanted was to let her down.

"I suppose I could manage to stay awake for a couple of hours. But if I do crap out, you can't get mad at me for falling asleep."

"Deal," Taylor said with a grin. "I get to pick the movie."

"No cop movies," Callie said as she got up from the table and followed her out to the living room. "I hate cop movies."

Callie sat against the arm of the couch while Taylor rented a movie for them to watch digitally on the television. *Ghostbusters* wouldn't have been Callie's first choice, but it would do for a mindless couple of hours.

"Can I ask you something?" Taylor said, her finger poised above the button on the remote that would start the movie.

"Okay," Callie said, feeling a bit apprehensive about what might be asked. She put her elbow on the arm of the couch and rested her head in her hand as she watched Taylor.

"The doctor called you Calliope," she said, meeting Callie's eyes. The intensity of her gaze almost caused Callie's heart to stop beating.

"Yeah, David's an ass. I've known him since elementary school. But it is not my name," she said with a grin. "He just does it because he knows it irritates the hell out of me."

"Then what is your name? I mean, what's Callie short for?"

"It isn't short for anything." She couldn't believe Quinn had never told her about how they got their names. They'd been working together for what seemed like forever to Callie. She sighed and realized any story concerning their father would likely be a tale Quinn wouldn't want to convey to anyone. "Our father wanted boys. He wanted nothing more than to name a son after himself. I guess when Beth, and then Meg were born, he figured there was still time. When Quinn came along, he started feeling as though his time was running out to try for a boy. His middle name was Quinn. Apparently, by the time I showed up, he knew he wasn't going to have a son, at least not with our mother. His first name was Calvin. So they named me Callie. It really isn't short for anything. My birth certificate says Callie Burke. No middle name. Just Callie. About three years later, he left us to presumably find a younger woman who could give him the son he always dreamed of."

"So you might have siblings out there you don't know about?"

"I'm sure I do. I just hope none of them are brothers. He deserves nothing other than daughters after abandoning all of us."

"That would just be cruel for someone who wanted a son so badly," Taylor said after a moment. Callie was about to get defensive when she realized Taylor was trying not to laugh. "But it would serve him right."

"Do you have any siblings?" Callie found herself wanting to know more about Taylor. Andrea really hadn't talked much about Taylor's life before they'd met, so she knew things like her favorite foods and her favorite color. And Andrea loved telling Callie about all the fun things they did together. Like skydiving. Now there was something Callie would never do. Who in their right mind would jump out of an airplane? Of course, she didn't understand what would make someone run into a burning building either.

"Nope, I'm an only child. My parents always told me they achieved perfection with me, and why would they want to risk anything less by trying for another?" She sighed, and then shook her head with a sad smile. Callie ached to hold her hand. "In reality, my mother couldn't have any more children."

"I'm sorry." Callie instinctively tried to raise her right arm to take Taylor's hand, but stopped when she felt a stab of pain that made her feel like she'd been shot again. She held her breath for a moment until the pain subsided, and was grateful Taylor was staring at the blank television screen and hadn't seen the look of pain she was certain had been on her face.

"Don't be. I sometimes wonder what it would be like to have a sister or brother, I mean, I see how close you and Quinn are, and I can't imagine having someone who knows me so well. But growing up it never bothered me. I didn't have to share my parents with anyone else, and I'll admit I was a little spoiled."

"No, you?" Callie asked, her tone teasing. She pushed her toe against Taylor's leg, and then cleared her throat, realizing it might not have been a smart thing to do. "I never would have guessed, what with them cooking Thanksgiving dinner and bringing it to your house."

"Shut up and watch the movie," Taylor said with a quick backhand to Callie's thigh.

Callie tensed slightly and found she wasn't able to concentrate on the movie for the first ten minutes because all she could think was *oh my God, Taylor touched me.*

How pathetic could she be?

Chapter Seven

Taylor woke up around three in the morning to find they'd both fallen asleep at some point during the movie. Callie was curled up in what looked to be an incredibly uncomfortable position on just one cushion of the couch. Blaze was stretched out beyond just the center cushion, his head resting on Callie's calves and his rear end pressed against Taylor where she was still in an upright position against the arm on her side of the couch.

He lifted his head when she placed a hand on Blaze's side, but when she asked him if he needed to go outside, he simply looked at her as though she'd lost her mind before he put his head back on Callie's calves. Callie stirred then, but she didn't wake up. Taylor watched her for a few moments in the blue hazy light coming from the television screen.

She looked so peaceful in sleep. Innocent, almost. Taylor felt a longing she hadn't experienced since Andrea's death, and she'd be lying if she said it didn't bother her. Andrea had been the love of her life, and she'd always thought there would never be another. Of course what she was feeling now wasn't love—how could it be? She barely knew Callie. But there was definitely a sexual pull toward her, and that was something she'd thought she *knew* she'd never feel again.

It was stupid to feel as though she'd be cheating on Andrea if she were to start dating again. She knew it intellectually, but her heart wasn't quite there yet. She sighed and rested her head on the back of the couch.

If she were to give in to her desires, would Andrea be okay with it being her best friend? Or would it be the ultimate betrayal? She chastised herself as she stole another glance at Callie. *It's never going to happen. According to what Andrea had said, Callie's into one-night stands, and I'm not wired that way. Not to mention the fact she's a cop. And a reckless one to boot.*

She shook her head and stood before going to the hall closet and pulling out a blanket. She didn't see any reason to wake her up at this point. She put the blanket over her, taking care to not cover Blaze's head, because he absolutely hated being under the covers. She brushed a lock of hair from Callie's forehead and let her fingers linger there a little too long. She turned the TV off and headed to her bedroom.

❖

The next time she woke up, it was to the sound of Blaze barking. In the backyard. At seven o'clock in the morning. On a holiday. The neighbors would be pissed.

"Shit," Taylor muttered as she threw the covers off and hurried out to the kitchen and opened the door. He came running full speed and almost knocked her over. He didn't like being left out there alone. She went to the living room to tell Callie as much, but she wasn't there. She scratched her head and walked back down the hall. She wasn't in her exercise room, nor was she in the guest bathroom. She walked back into her bedroom and noticed the door to the master bathroom was closed.

She jumped when she heard something hit the door rather hard. She knocked twice and tried the handle when there was no response. It was locked. Jesus, what if she'd fallen over and knocked herself out? She really didn't want to have to call a locksmith out on a holiday just to get her bathroom door open. She didn't even want to guess what the cost might be.

"Callie?" she said as she knocked again. "Callie, are you all right?"

She heard the door being unlocked and then it opened slightly. She tentatively pushed it open, hoping she wasn't going to see blood anywhere. She let out a sigh of relief when she saw Callie standing at the sink.

"What happened? I heard a loud bang from in here."

"Oh, that was just me losing my balance and falling into the door," Callie said as she met her eyes in the mirror. She grinned a bit sheepishly. "I was trying to take my shirt off so I could maybe clean myself a little bit, and I couldn't manage it. No worries. At least I didn't land on my bad shoulder, so it could have been much worse."

"Do you need help?"

"You want to undress me?"

Callie's grin turned from embarrassed to something Taylor couldn't quite identify. All she knew was it caused a strange feeling deep in her belly she wasn't sure she liked. Nor was she sure she *didn't* like it. She felt the heat in her cheeks as Callie continued looking at her in the mirror.

"You're here so I can help you," Taylor finally said without committing one way or the other to the question she was sure was meant to embarrass her. "So if you need help, you should just ask."

"Nice way to avoid answering the question," Callie said with a chuckle. She turned and leaned against the counter as she studied her. "I'm willing to bet you hadn't thought this through very well before offering to let me stay here with you. I'm sure things like helping me dress and undress weren't high on your list of things to do."

"You're right. I hadn't thought it through." Taylor saw no point in lying to her about it. "But you're here, and I'm here, so if you need help with something, ask. All right?"

"And if I need help bathing?"

"Do you?" Taylor hoped to God the answer would be no. She wasn't sure she'd be able to deal with a naked Callie in her bathroom.

"Probably not, but I'm not sure how easy washing my hair will be with just my left hand."

"Then how about I help you get your shirt off, then when you're done bathing, come to the kitchen and we'll wash your hair in the sink?"

Callie held her gaze for a moment before finally nodding. Taylor took in a deep breath before stepping toward her and helping her to get out of her sweatshirt. She kept her eyes averted as she did so, and neither one of them spoke other than to give directions to the other.

"Thank you," Callie said when Taylor turned to leave the room. "I know having me here is probably uncomfortable for you, but I appreciate the help."

Taylor simply nodded, but still refused to turn and look at her. She pulled the door closed behind her and finally let out the breath she was holding when she closed her eyes and leaned against the wall for support. She wondered if Callie knew the truth of her last statement. It was definitely uncomfortable having her here, but it had nothing to do with her specifically. It had everything to do with the fact she'd not had anyone in her house overnight since Andrea died. And there'd certainly been no one in her bedroom—or the master bath—since then.

❖

Callie struggled to do what she needed to do. A soapy washcloth and a tub full of water seemed to be the easiest way to bathe without getting the stitches in her shoulder wet. She hadn't taken a bath since she was about ten, which was when she began taking showers instead. Drying off when she was finished proved to be a challenge with only one arm. It took a considerable amount of time, but she breathed a sigh of relief when she'd finally finished.

After a couple of attempts to put on a clean sweatshirt proved futile, she admitted to herself she needed help. She hated being forced to rely on other people. She'd been independent and self-reliant for as long as she could remember.

She smiled when she remembered the way Taylor had tried so hard to not look at her when she was helping to remove her shirt. It was obvious to Callie she hadn't been averting her eyes as a sign of respect to her, but instead Taylor's attraction to her was evident. Anytime her hand inadvertently touched Callie's skin she'd pulled it away as if she'd been burned.

She wondered why Andrea had felt the need to tell her Taylor didn't like her. Taylor denied ever saying anything of the kind. Was it possible Andrea knew Taylor found her attractive and it was her way of keeping them apart? Callie pondered the notion that Andrea might have told Taylor the same thing about her.

A knock on the door startled her, and she managed to place a towel over her naked chest before telling Taylor she could come in.

"You've been in here for quite a long time," Taylor said. "I was just checking to make sure you were all right."

"I'm fine." Callie smiled and leaned against the counter. She held the shirt out to her. "I'm afraid I can't manage this though. I'm sorry."

"There's no need to apologize," Taylor said. She took the shirt and began helping. Callie decided to take mercy on her and left the towel in place. It would be easy enough to remove it after she was sufficiently covered. "Grab your shampoo and we'll get your hair washed."

"What time are your parents going to be here?"

"They said about noon." Taylor chuckled. "Which means they'll probably be here around eleven thirty."

"For my mother it would mean twelve thirty. I swear she's going to be late to her own funeral," Callie said. She hesitated as she picked up the shampoo bottle she'd left on the counter. "Are you sure it's okay for me to be here today?"

"I'm sure." Taylor nodded and motioned for her to follow. "Just don't be surprised when they assume we're dating. For some reason they didn't believe me when I said we weren't."

"Would it be easier if we let them think we were?" Callie winced when the words left her mouth, and she was grateful Taylor was ahead of her, so she couldn't see how much she regretted what she'd said. As it was, Taylor's step faltered, and then she stopped in the hallway to the kitchen and turned around.

"What exactly are you suggesting?" She didn't seem to be upset at the idea, which for some reason emboldened Callie.

"I just thought maybe it would make them feel better to think you aren't alone." When Taylor didn't respond, Callie decided to elaborate. "I mean, obviously whoever you've been in relationships with in the past three and a half years hasn't worked out. Maybe they'd like to know you're not sitting around by yourself."

"I haven't been in a relationship since Andrea died," Taylor said, her voice tight.

Callie felt like her feet were too heavy to move as she watched Taylor disappear into the kitchen. How could it be possible she hadn't been with anyone in over three years? Callie was certain it wasn't because no one had asked her out. She was too beautiful to not have women trying to date her. Men too, for that matter. No, maybe no relationships, but she must have dated, and simply not found anyone she liked enough to be with long-term. That was something Callie could understand.

She shook her head and forced her feet to carry her down the hall. She shouldn't be thinking about Taylor this way. It was becoming glaringly apparent she was trying to isolate herself from the world to a certain extent, and Callie didn't have the energy to deal with someone who had no desire to live their life to the fullest.

It was almost eleven thirty when Quinn called, and Callie took her phone to the kitchen and looked out the window above the sink as she answered it.

"Happy Thanksgiving, Sis," she said by way of greeting.

"To you too," Quinn replied. "I'm sorry I didn't call you yesterday, but Meg dragged us out grocery shopping for today's feast, and you know how much I hate grocery stores. Before I knew it, it was too late to call."

"Don't worry about it. How is everyone there?"

"Good, but how are you, Cal? You scared the hell out of us, you know."

"Scared the hell out of myself." Callie chuckled.

"I'm glad you're okay." Quinn sounded a little choked up, and it made Callie happy to know there were people who cared so much about her. "Are you behaving yourself?"

"For the most part," she answered, remembering Taylor helping her to remove her shirt earlier.

"I'll still have a job when I get back?"

"Well, I can't promise anything." Callie watched as a light snow began to fall. "But I can assure you I'm being my usual charming self."

"That's a bit alarming." Quinn laughed. "But at least you're housebroken. You are housebroken, right?"

"Of course I am. I haven't wet the bed since I was twelve, I think," Callie allowed a small smile. "Which is better than you did, I might add."

"What can I say? I was a sound sleeper when I was a teenager."

"You're still a sound sleeper," Callie said. "Who are you trying to fool? I should ask Grace if you've wet the bed lately."

"Okay, truce," Quinn said with a chuckle. "What are you doing for the holiday? Didn't you say your partner and his wife invited you to their house?"

"Yeah, I only said that so Mom wouldn't worry about me being alone," Callie admitted. "Taylor's parents are coming here for dinner today."

"I kind of figured you fibbed about your partner. I haven't seen Bob and Eleanor in years. Tell them I said hello." Quinn said something to someone on her end of the line, then came back. "Mom wants to talk to you. I'll see you on Sunday, all right? I'm not sure what time it will be though."

"I'll be here waiting." Callie grinned. Where else would she be? It wasn't like she had her car, and even if she did, she wasn't sure she'd be able to drive it with one hand.

"Hey, Cal?" Quinn said quietly. "I love you."

"I love you, too," Callie said, surprised at the rush of emotion she felt. It wasn't like either one of them to be sentimental, but she figured it was a good thing to put words to your feelings once in a while.

"Callie," her mother said after Quinn evidently handed her the phone. "I'm so happy you're okay. I was worried sick the other night after Quinn got the call about what had happened."

"I'm fine, Mom," she said with a soft smile. "You aren't getting rid of me so easily."

"Grace wants to say hello."

"No, Mom, wait," Callie said as she watched a car pull into Taylor's driveway. "I have to go. Taylor's parents are here. Tell Grace and Meg and everyone else hello for me, and give them all a hug, okay? I'll see you soon."

"Okay," she said. "Thank Taylor for me for taking care of you."

She finally managed to end the call at the same time the doorbell rang. Taylor stuck her head in the kitchen on her way to answer it.

"Everything okay?" she asked.

"Fine." Callie smiled. She took a deep breath and tried to prepare herself to meet Taylor's parents.

Chapter Eight

You two can sit out here and watch the parade while we get the food heated up," Taylor's mother said to Callie and Taylor's father. Callie wasn't about to argue. Of course she wouldn't be able to help much anyway, even if she'd wanted to.

"Are you a football fan, Callie?" Taylor's father asked when they were alone.

"Yes, sir, Mr. Fletcher."

"Please, it's Bob," he said with a smile. His eyes dropped to her shoulder, and she wiped her left hand on her pant leg, surprised her palm was actually sweating. "First time?"

"Excuse me?" Callie asked, wondering exactly what he was referring to.

"Being shot." He had the television remote in his hand but set it down on the coffee table without turning the set on.

"It is, yes," she answered, not minding in the least he chose not to turn the parade on. She hated parades, and they were even worse on TV.

"I was shot twice, myself," he said.

"Are you a police officer?" Callie was a little surprised. Why wouldn't Taylor have said something about her sharing a profession with her father?

"No, retired FBI."

"Wow. Taylor neglected to mention that."

"I'm not surprised. When she was younger, she was proud of her special agent dad," he said with a soft smile. He looked at her then and shook his head. "But after she lost Andrea, her opinion of people who choose to risk their lives every day changed dramatically. She was relieved when I retired earlier this year."

Callie nodded as though she completely understood, but in reality, she struggled to grasp why Taylor would think so little of all people in high-risk jobs. Obviously, it had hit her hard when Andrea died, Callie already knew that, but could it possibly be the reason why she didn't like her? Callie really couldn't grasp that way of thinking.

"I always tell her somebody has to do those jobs," Bob said after a moment. "Which she says is fine, but she doesn't have to surround herself with the people who do them."

"I had no idea she felt that way," Callie said. "But I guess it helps to explain why she seems so irritated with me about having gotten shot."

"She'll get over it," he said, sounding more confident than Callie felt. "She told me, and I also read a bit online about what happened. While I agree with her assessment that you should have waited for your partner, you didn't really do anything wrong. She'll understand at some point."

He picked up the remote again and turned on the parade. Callie tuned it out and became lost in her own thoughts. If Taylor disliked her because of her profession, then there wasn't anything she could do about it. She wasn't going to stop doing the job she loved. She'd never had to deal with someone not liking her because of her job. Well, except for murderers, but who cared what they thought? She closed her eyes for a moment and sighed.

"Can I get you something to drink?" she asked Bob, mostly because she wanted one, and she couldn't have one because of her pain medication. Maybe she could live vicariously through Bob.

"I could go for a beer, but I can get it myself," he said. He started to get up, but she stopped him.

"No, it isn't a problem," she assured him. She patted Blaze on the head as he jumped onto the couch to take her seat. "Be right back."

❖

"She seems nice," Taylor's mother said while she and Taylor were heating up the food. Taylor shook her head and turned to look at her. She'd known this was going to happen. "And she's very attractive, too."

"Mom, I told you we aren't dating."

"I know you did, dear, but she still seems nice."

"I suppose." Taylor sighed and opened the oven so her mother could put the turkey in. Yes, Callie did seem nice. Taylor just wished Callie wasn't succeeding in ruining every negative thing she'd thought of her over the years.

"Maybe you should be dating her."

"Mom, please."

"What? I worry about you, dear." Her mother turned to face her and put her hands on her hips. Taylor thought she looked as though she were ready to brawl. "Your father and I just want you to be happy, Taylor."

"Please, just stop." Taylor faced her mother, mirroring her stance, hands on hips. "I am happy, okay? Can you please let it go?"

"How can you possibly be happy when you have no one to share your life with?"

"I don't need another person to make my life complete." Taylor was well aware Callie and her father were just in the next room, and she was doing her best to keep her voice down. Her mother's infuriating persistence wasn't making it easy for her. "And besides, like I told you on the phone the other day, I don't really know her. Hell, I'm not sure I even like her."

"Then why would you offer to let her stay here with you?"

"She was Andrea's best friend. And I didn't want to make Quinn cut her trip short."

"So instead, you changed your own holiday plans."

"Jesus, Mom," Taylor said as she ran her hand through her hair in frustration. "You live less than two hours from here. Quinn is in Philadelphia. Callie has no other family here. I didn't think it would be a big deal."

"It's not, dear," her mother said with a sly smile. "I'm just pointing out that if you truly didn't like her, you wouldn't have even considered taking on this responsibility."

Taylor wanted to argue, but she knew her mother was right. Even at forty-two, she was still pissed off when her mother reminded her of the fact she was more intuitive than Taylor wanted to give her credit for.

"The food smells wonderful," Callie said as she walked into the kitchen. She was smiling, and Taylor wondered how much of their conversation she'd heard.

"It does, doesn't it?" her mother asked. "We'll be ready to eat in a few minutes."

"Your dad wanted a beer," Callie said as she opened the fridge.

"Seriously? And he sent you in here to get it for him?" Taylor couldn't believe he'd do such a thing to the only person in the house who was injured. She headed for the living room, but Callie stopped her.

"I asked if he wanted anything," she said. "I offered, Taylor. He didn't *send* me in here."

"Oh." Taylor swore at herself under her breath for thinking he would. "Okay."

"I need a little help getting the cap off the bottle though."

"Here, I've got it." Taylor's mother grabbed the bottle opener from the drawer and popped the top off for her. "Aren't you having one?"

"Mom, she's on painkillers," Taylor said. She gave Callie a tight smile as they passed each other on Callie's way back to the living room.

"Thank you, Mrs. Fletcher," Callie said over her shoulder.

"It's Eleanor, please." When Callie was gone, her mother winked at Taylor. "Polite, attractive, and enchantingly charming, to boot. A very good combination."

"Please stop." Taylor opened the microwave and removed the stuffing so she could heat up the green bean casserole. "Just…stop."

"What? If I were twenty years younger and swung that way…"

"Oh, my God," Taylor said as she hung her head and felt her cheeks flush. "Have you always been this embarrassing? I don't remember you being this embarrassing while I was growing up."

"Yes, dear, I have," she answered with a pat to Taylor's forearm. "But I used to be a bit more subtle about it."

"So, Callie, football. I assume you're a Bills fan?" Taylor's father asked after they'd all stuffed themselves.

"Yes, sir, I am," she answered. "Even though I would dearly love to root for a team that might make the playoffs someday."

"I told you to stop with the sir," he said with a shake of his head. "Call me Bob."

"You two go watch football," Eleanor told them. "Taylor and I will clean up."

"Come on, before they change their minds," Bob said as he stood.

Callie wanted to offer to help, but Taylor motioned for her to follow Bob. The conversation during dinner had been light and easy enough, but Callie had heard a bit of what Taylor and Eleanor were saying before she'd gotten the beer for Bob. Taylor didn't like her. She'd known this, but had hoped since yesterday they'd forged some kind of friendship. Obviously, she'd been wrong.

"So, Detroit or Minnesota in the first game?" Bob asked.

"If the Vikings hadn't lost five out of the last six, I'd pick them, but I think the Lions are going to win." Callie reached into her pocket and pulled out a pain pill. After swallowing it, she turned to Bob and smiled. "And before you ask, the Cowboys are going to win the later game. Washington doesn't stand a chance."

"I agree wholeheartedly," he said with a chuckle. They settled in as the pre-game ended, but it seemed Bob had something on his mind. He lowered his voice as he leaned a little closer to her and glanced toward the kitchen. "Can I ask you a personal question?"

"Sure," she said, a bit uneasy. That was one question she hated hearing.

"Taylor denies it, but are you two dating?"

"No," she answered with a chuckle. "We aren't."

"Damn it. I figured as much, given what you do for a living, but I was hoping. I think you'd be good for her." He straightened again and turned his attention back to the TV. "We've been worried about her ever since Andrea died. As far as I know, she hasn't dated at all since then."

Callie didn't know what to say. She stared at the television, but she wasn't seeing what she was watching. Her mind was filled with Taylor, and she knew it shouldn't be.

"It's not because I don't want to."

He looked at her, and she cringed at the realization she'd said those words out loud. He nodded with a knowing smile.

"Have you asked her?"

"No," Callie said, looking at the TV again. "Our relationship is a bit complicated, I guess you could say."

"How long have you known her?"

"Since before she met Andrea, but again, it's complicated. I was friends with Andrea, but I never really spent time with the two of them. I don't think Taylor really likes me, if I'm being honest."

"Taylor likes everyone." He waved her comment off. After a moment, he looked at her again. "Unless they do something to hurt her. Have you?"

"No," Callie said, sounding more defensive than she'd meant to. "Not that I know of."

"Then you should ask her out. What's the worst that could happen?"

"Maybe," she said, mostly because she didn't want to talk about it any longer. The worst that could happen? She could laugh at her, or kick her out before Quinn got home. Hell, she could fire Quinn for that matter. No, asking Taylor out was not something she would do anytime soon.

❖

"Thank you again for dinner. It was wonderful," Callie said when Bob and Eleanor were putting their coats on. She had a hand on her stomach, thinking she should have passed on the second—and the third—slice of pumpkin pie. It had been so good though.

"It was our pleasure, Callie," Eleanor said with a smile. "Hopefully, we can do it again sometime soon."

Taylor shook her head slightly as she stared at her mother. Callie almost laughed at her stern expression, but somehow managed to stifle it. She had a feeling laughing would have been a bad idea right then.

"Drive carefully," Taylor said as she opened the door for them to leave.

"Subtlety never was your strong point, was it?" Bob chuckled before leaning in and giving Taylor a kiss on the cheek.

"Nope." Taylor hugged Eleanor and then they were gone. She shut the door and leaned her forehead against it for a moment before turning and facing Callie. "You certainly made an impression with them."

"Is that a good thing or a bad thing?"

"Oh, I'd say it was good. At least for them."

"You never told me your father was in the FBI."

"It just never came up." Taylor shrugged like it was no big deal. "Was he interrogating you about dating me?"

"Actually, yeah, he did a little bit." Callie moved aside to allow Taylor to pass on her way to the living room.

"I hope you told him to mind his own business."

"Um, no. Not exactly." She knew she should have lied and told her she did, but lying wasn't really something she did. Not to mention she absolutely sucked at it. Her mother had always been able to see right through any lie she'd attempted to tell.

"What did you tell him?" Taylor looked worried, and Callie thought she was cute with that particular expression.

"I said we weren't dating, but I also told him it wasn't because I didn't want to."

"Oh, for God's sake, Callie." Taylor sighed and leaned forward, her forearms resting on her thighs. "You know that's never going to happen."

"Why not?" Callie tried to not sound disappointed, but she didn't think she'd done a very good job of it.

"For one thing, you told *him* you wanted to date me, but you've never said anything about it to me, and for another thing, I don't date first responders anymore."

"What?" Callie decided not to disclose that Bob had already told her as much, albeit in not those exact words. "I'll admit I probably should have actually asked you out before saying something to your father about it. But technically, I'm not a first responder you know. I'm a homicide detective, and I only get called to the scene of a crime after a murder has been committed."

"And yet here you are, recovering from a gunshot wound. How do you explain that?" Taylor stood and looked down at her. "I'll tell you how. You were chasing a *murder* suspect who was desperate to get away. You can't tell me you don't put your life on the line every day you go to work. But you know what? None of it matters because according to you, I don't even like you."

Callie stared at the wall across the room as Taylor stormed out. She flinched when she heard the door to the bedroom slam shut. She let her head fall back against the couch. That conversation certainly hadn't gone the way she thought it might. She hadn't expected a date out of it, but she'd hoped maybe they could have shared a laugh.

Blaze came to her and sat on the floor by her feet, his chin resting on her thigh. He looked up at her, his big brown eyes looking sad. She scratched him behind the ears and sighed.

"I might not be here much longer, boy," she said. He lifted his head and licked her arm. "Maybe you should put in a good word for me. I think I could use all the help I can get as far as your mom is concerned."

CHAPTER NINE

Taylor woke up the next morning feeling even more like an ass than she had the night before. She put her pillow over her head and buried herself under the covers. She'd told Callie she could sleep in her bed and she'd take the couch, yet here it was, two days later, and both nights Taylor had slept in her own bed. After a few moments, she threw the covers off and walked dejectedly to the bathroom.

Once showered and dressed, she felt a little better, but there was no doubt she was still an ass. And Blaze had slept in the living room the last two nights. Even he knew she was an ass. She wouldn't blame him if he liked Callie more than her at this point.

"Good morning," Callie said when Taylor walked into the kitchen. Taylor went straight to the coffee pot and poured herself a cup. She sounded downright cheerful. "I let Blaze out and gave him some food."

"Thank you." Taylor was surprised, and she could tell Callie knew it. "For taking care of Blaze *and* the coffee."

"You're welcome."

"I need to apologize for last night."

"Don't worry about it." Callie stood and took her cup to the sink just as Taylor sat across from her. "But if it's all the same to you, I think I'm just going to go on home today. This obviously isn't working out very well."

"What?" Taylor turned in her seat to better see her, thinking she was probably joking. The expression on her face told Taylor she was not. Quinn would never forgive her if she allowed Callie to go home on her own. "You're not going anywhere."

"Come on, Taylor," she said, sitting once again. "I heard some of the conversation between you and your mother yesterday. I heard you tell her why you were letting me stay here. You also told her you weren't sure you even liked me."

Taylor stared at her a moment, trying to decide if there was any point in lying to her about it. She sighed and shook her head. She'd heard it right, so what good could possibly come from denying it?

"I'm sorry," Taylor said, almost surprised to realize she meant it. In reality, what reason was there to not like Callie? She was polite, her parents liked her, she'd taken care of Blaze and made coffee this morning. You could never underestimate the power of coffee. On the surface, Callie seemed to be the perfect woman. She pushed the thought to the back of her mind, refusing to think about it. How would Callie feel if she found out Taylor had always found her attractive?

"Thank you for not trying to put a spin on it," Callie said.

"I only told her what I did because I didn't want to talk about it with her."

"Now see, that," Callie said, pointing a finger at her and moving it in a circle, "is a spin."

"It's the truth." Taylor wanted to stop herself from speaking, but it didn't seem possible. Her brain had somehow disconnected from her mouth. "I don't *not* like you, okay?"

"A double negative?" Callie grinned. "So you're saying you *do* like me."

It was a statement, not a question, and Taylor could have just left it alone, but then again, her mouth apparently still hadn't engaged with her brain.

"Maybe. The jury's still out." Taylor went to the coffee pot to refill her cup, mostly so Callie couldn't see her smiling. "Unless, of course, the polite and charming Callie I've seen the past two days has all been an act."

"Nope, what you see is what you get."

"Quinn said the same thing about herself when I met her."

"She and I are so alike it scares me sometimes. Pretty sure it scares her too. And our mother? It terrifies her." Callie grinned, and Taylor couldn't help but return it.

"You'll stay here until Quinn gets back on Sunday?"

"Yeah, I'll stay." Callie sat again and winced at the stab of pain that went through her shoulder when she accidentally banged her arm on the table.

"Are you all right?" Taylor asked, rushing to her side.

Callie nodded and pretended not to notice Taylor's hand firmly on her thigh as she knelt down beside her. She was afraid Taylor would move away if she acknowledged the touch in any way because Callie didn't think Taylor was even aware she was touching her.

"I'm fine," she answered through clenched teeth.

"Sure you are, tough guy." Taylor squeezed her thigh and let go, leaving Callie to feel the loss immediately. "I'll get you a pain pill."

"Fuck, Burke, get a grip," Callie muttered under her breath when Taylor left the room. *She just admitted she might like you. No reason to read anything into it.*

Callie watched Taylor as she came back into the kitchen and went to get her a glass of water. When she got back to the table and handed her the pill, Callie took it without any argument.

She wasn't going to deny she needed it. Acting tough was one thing, but acting tough to the detriment of your own well-being was another. After she swallowed the pill, she looked up at Taylor and grinned.

"So, you think I'm charming?"

"And egotistical, apparently." Taylor shook her head and took the chair across from her. "My mother was the one who used the word. I was just repeating it."

"Oh."

"You don't need to sound so disappointed." Taylor laughed and reached over to touch her hand. When Callie looked down, Taylor pulled her hand away. "Sorry."

"For what?" Callie asked. "You haven't done anything you need to be sorry for."

"I shouldn't have touched you."

"Why? It doesn't have to mean anything, you know." Of course, that didn't mean Callie didn't want it to mean something. She just didn't want Taylor to freak out about it. "Friends touch like that sometimes."

"Friends?" Taylor sounded surprised. "I'm not sure we're there quite yet."

"But we're on our way, right?" Callie stared at her hand as she drummed her fingers on the tabletop. When Taylor didn't answer, she looked up and met her eyes. "I mean, if I'm traveling down this road of getting to know each other better all by my lonesome, I think you should tell me now."

"You aren't," Taylor said, but she looked away before saying it. Callie leaned forward and took her hand, holding a little tighter than she needed to because she thought Taylor would try to pull away.

"Listen, I know it's been over three years, but Andrea was my best friend. And you were her wife." Callie paused, but

Taylor still refused to look at her. "We both dealt with her loss alone. Maybe it's time to talk about it."

"There's nothing to talk about."

"Isn't there?" She squeezed Taylor's fingers briefly. "For all this time I've been convinced that not only do you hate me, but you also blamed me for her death."

"I never blamed you. I never blamed anyone."

"She ran back into a burning building to save a child. Sounds like something a reckless idiot like me would do, don't you think?"

Callie felt a tear running down her cheek, and she wanted to wipe it away, but Taylor chose that moment to look at her, and she closed her other hand around Callie's, holding her in place. Callie couldn't look at her. She hung her head and took a deep breath. Taylor held her hand tightly until Callie finally met her eyes.

"She ran back in to save a little girl because that was who she was," Taylor said quietly. "She died doing what she loved. I knew every time she walked out the door there was a chance she wouldn't be coming home. Knowing it could happen didn't make it any easier to deal with when it did. It was something we both knew was possible, and we talked about it many times. I've had such a hard time dealing with it because we had a fight before she left for work."

"I know." Callie pulled her hand away and wiped the tears from her cheeks. "She told me. She wanted a baby and you didn't."

"Jesus, did everyone know?"

"I'm pretty sure she didn't tell anyone but me."

"I called her to apologize for the awful things I said, but she didn't answer. I left a message, but she didn't call me back. I don't think she ever got it." Taylor began to cry, and Callie got to her feet to go kneel in front of her.

"Hey, Taylor, she did get the message," Callie said. Taylor looked at her, her eyes overflowing with tears.

"Why didn't she call me back?"

"She said she was going to."

"Why didn't you tell me?" Taylor looked pissed, but then her expression softened. "I'm sorry. Why would you have? We weren't exactly talking at the time."

"I thought she'd done it. When everything happened, it sort of slipped my mind." Callie reached up and brushed a lock of hair away that had fallen in front of Taylor's eyes. She let her hand linger on her cheek, and Taylor leaned into her touch for a moment. "She didn't die with the argument being her last memory of you."

Taylor closed her eyes and cried for a few moments, and Callie wasn't sure what to do. Finally, she stood to go back to her seat, but Taylor stood as well, and embraced her carefully, so as not to hurt her shoulder.

"Thank you," she said into Callie's ear. The subtlety of breath in such a sensitive area caused a shiver to run through Callie. "Thank you for telling me."

"I'm just sorry I didn't think to tell you sooner."

Taylor pulled away and wiped the tears from her cheeks. Callie could tell by the look in her eye Taylor's imaginary wall had gone back up between them, so she let out a breath and went to get more coffee. At least it was a start. With time, maybe they could actually become friends.

CHAPTER TEN

Taylor was happy she had to go to work later in the afternoon. While the closeness she and Callie shared earlier had been nice, and it made her feel infinitely better to learn Andrea had indeed gotten her message that day before she died, she was finding it harder to keep the distance between the two of them. Her nerves felt raw, and she was having trouble remembering she had no desire to be with anyone who put their life on the line on a daily basis.

And it was pissing her off that she kept thinking about Callie. About how good Callie had felt in her arms. And especially about how badly she'd wanted to kiss her before finally pulling away from her. She pulled her phone out and scrolled to Callie's name, smiling when she saw it. Callie had entered her number into the phone so she'd have it, and then Taylor called her so she would have hers too.

"Damn it, I've got to stop thinking about her," she muttered as she stood up from her desk. She wasn't really needed at the bar since the majority of their business was college students, and most of them had gone home for the holiday weekend, but she needed something to do in order to keep her mind busy.

Camille had everything under control, as there were only three people sitting at the bar. There were a couple others playing pool, and a handful of customers at tables. She sighed. She'd thought about giving Camille the night off, but it was hard to gauge what the night was going to be like, especially on the Friday of a holiday weekend.

A quick glance at the digital clock on the cash register told her it was only ten o'clock. She sighed and walked behind the bar. There was a woman at the end of the bar who was waving in Camille's direction to get another drink, but Taylor decided to take the customer's order.

"I've got it," she said as she walked past her temporary head bartender. She couldn't wait for Quinn to get back from Philadelphia. Camille was great, but Taylor had known Quinn for more than fifteen years. The easy rapport they shared was comforting, and made slow nights like this go by much quicker. She smiled at the woman as she picked up her empty glass. "What can I get you?"

"How about your phone number?" she replied with a grin Taylor was sure she thought was sexy, but to Taylor it just came off as creepy. Seriously creepy. She was attractive enough, but Taylor wasn't interested. Especially with such a lame pickup line. And then there was the creepy factor to consider.

"What are you drinking?" Taylor hoped rephrasing the question would put an end to her being hit on.

"Come on, honey, I could show you a good time," she said, trying on a pout, which again, Taylor found unsettling. "Just give me a chance. I promise you won't regret it."

"I'm not available," Taylor said with a shake of her head. She was regretting her decision to wait on this woman though. She held the glass up one more time. "What are you drinking?"

"Rum and Coke," she said, looking defeated. Taylor could only hope it was the end of it.

"Taylor," Camille called from a few feet away. "I'm going in the back for more ice."

Taylor waved her acknowledgment as she prepared the drink for her obnoxious admirer. When she set the glass in front of her, the woman grabbed her by the wrist. It was becoming obvious she'd already had too much to drink, so Taylor used her other hand to grab her wrist and twisted it while simultaneously squeezing as hard as she could.

"What the fuck?" the woman said loud enough for every person in the bar to look at them. At least it had been enough to make her let go.

"You need to leave." Taylor picked up the drink and dumped it into the sink in front of her before the woman even had a chance to stop her. She was a little frightened by her, but she refused to let it show, and she resisted the urge to rub her wrist. "Now."

"You hurt me," she said, but made no move to vacate her seat. She was rubbing her wrist when a rather large gentleman walked up behind her.

"Is there a problem?" he asked Taylor.

"She twisted my arm," the woman answered before Taylor could.

Taylor met the man's eyes, and she almost laughed when he rolled them in response.

"If she did, then you probably deserved it. She asked you to leave. I suggest you do it. Now." He placed his hand under her arm, near her elbow, and forced her to stand up. Taylor watched as he led her toward the front door.

"This isn't over, you bitch!" the woman shouted just before the door closed behind them.

Taylor took a deep breath and shook her head, trying to calm herself. She smiled at the man as he walked back to the bar.

"Are you okay?" he asked.

"What happened?" Camille came up beside Taylor and gently touched her arm.

"I'm fine, thank you," Taylor said.

"My name's Randy," he said, extending his hand across the bar. Taylor shook it and glanced at Camille.

"Give Randy and his friends their next round on the house."

"Thank you very much, but it isn't necessary," he said with a smile. He leaned across the bar. "I asked her for her name on the way out, so if she ever shows up and bothers you again, it's Sharon. At least that's what she told me."

"Thank you," Taylor said again. When he walked back to his friends, she explained to Camille what had gone on while she'd been busy getting ice.

"Jesus, Taylor, I thought there was something a little off about her when she walked in. I only served her one drink, I swear."

"Don't worry about it," Taylor said, sounding calmer than she felt. "Did she try to come on to you too?"

"No, she just sort of rubbed me the wrong way. I can't really explain it."

"Well, she's gone, so no harm done."

"Do you want me to call Callie?"

"What? Why? It's over."

"You don't know that," Camille said adamantly. "She could come back. Or she might be waiting outside for you to leave."

"We don't need to call Callie," she said with a shake of her head. All she needed was for Callie to think she couldn't take care of herself.

"I think we do." Camille crossed her arms and stared at her. "If you don't do it, I will."

"Seriously? Did Quinn give you pointers before she left?"

"Yep." Camille grinned. "And I'm staying until you leave because there's no way I'm letting you walk out of here by yourself."

"You do realize you work for me, right?" Taylor asked, trying her best not to smile at the protectiveness Camille was showing.

"Yep, and I intend to keep working for you, which is why you should be worried about that woman coming back."

Taylor walked away, a little upset at being told what to do, but at the same time grateful for Camille's assurances she wouldn't leave her alone here. She would do the same for Camille, so why should she expect anything less? She pulled her cell phone out of her pocket and pressed the button to call Callie.

"Hello, Taylor," she said when she answered. "Miss me already?"

"Your ego really is gigantic, isn't it?" she asked as she sat down at her desk. "I hope I didn't wake you up."

"Nope, Blaze and I are watching a hockey game." Callie must have heard something strange in her voice. "Is everything okay?"

"Yeah, I'm sure everything is fine, but Camille bullied me into calling you."

"Why?"

Taylor heard rustling on the other end of the line and imagined Callie sitting up on the couch and pushing Blaze to the floor.

"There was a woman here. She was drunk. I made her leave."

"What else?"

"She was pushy. She was coming on to me."

"Did she threaten you in any way?"

"Not really." Taylor wondered how much of a threat she really posed, since her parting shot was made while drunk. She'd probably go home, sleep it off, and forget it all by morning, so why even mention it to Callie?

"I'm coming down there."

"Callie, no," she said quickly, but she heard Callie say something to the dog as she was probably getting to her feet. "She's gone. There's a guy here who got rid of her, and Camille is going to stay until I close to walk me to the car. There's no need for you to come here."

There was a pause, and Taylor heard Callie let out what sounded like an exasperated sigh.

"Fine, but I'm going in with you tomorrow night."

"You don't need to come to work with me," Taylor said. She closed her eyes, put an elbow on the desk, and rested her chin in her hand. "You'd be bored out of your mind."

"You can let me be the judge of what I find boring, all right?"

Taylor felt a lump in her throat, and she only nodded her acquiescence, knowing Callie couldn't see it. To be honest, Taylor was more than a little worried about the woman—Sharon—coming back. But if it was going to happen, she was sure it would be tonight. The fact Callie wanted to protect her made her feel good, yet a tad uncomfortable at the same time. She didn't want anyone to think they needed to watch over her.

"Taylor?" Callie's voice was soft, and it sent a shiver through Taylor. She opened her eyes and did her best to compose herself.

"Yes, okay," she said, almost as quietly as Callie spoke. "I'm probably going to close early tonight because it's not busy. I'd be paying more for Camille to be here and the electricity than I'd be bringing in."

"Call me when you're leaving so if you aren't home ten minutes later, I'll know something happened and I'll call the police."

"Callie—"

"Please don't fight about it. Just humor me," Callie said.

"Okay," Taylor said, knowing it was pointless to argue. Especially if Callie was as much like Quinn as she claimed. "I'll call you."

"Thank you. And thank Camille for me."

They hung up, and Taylor felt her eyes well up with tears. The concern and care Callie showed reminded her so much of Andrea. She really didn't know what to do with the feelings she was starting to experience for the first time since Andrea died.

CHAPTER ELEVEN

Callie kept looking at her phone, knowing she hadn't missed a call, but wishing she'd thought to ask Taylor what time she might be closing for the night. It was almost midnight now, and she was starting to get a little antsy. It was clear Blaze could feel her anxiety because he hadn't slept since she'd hung up with Taylor almost an hour and a half earlier. He just sat there with his chin on her leg watching her intently and jumping at every sound he heard outside.

She should have just called a cab and gone to the bar as soon as Taylor told her what happened. She'd seen it too many times in her job. Harassment the victim was sure was no big deal, and the next thing they knew they had a stalker. Her pulse spiked at the thought of it happening to Taylor.

The phone in her hand vibrated before it actually rang, and she answered the call immediately.

"Taylor," she said in a strangled voice, feeling her heart pounding wildly. The adrenaline at the thought of anything happening to her was threatening to overwhelm her.

"I woke you up," Taylor said. "I knew I shouldn't have called you."

"I was awake," she answered, not daring to admit the fear she'd been feeling. "Just hanging out with my buddy, Blaze."

"Well, we're on our way out the door now. I should be there in a few."

"We'll be here waiting." Callie tried to sound calm, but wasn't sure she was pulling it off.

Ten minutes came and went, and Callie started to worry. Blaze whined as she reached for her phone again. Just before she finished entering the number for the Brockport Police, Blaze ran to the door, his tail wagging crazily, and he barked once before looking back at her. When Callie heard the key in the door, she set her phone back down and was finally able to relax for the first time since Taylor originally called her about the incident.

"Hello, my baby boy," Taylor said to Blaze when she finally managed to get past him and inside the house. She smiled at Callie and waved. "I'm home, safe and sound."

"I can see that," Callie answered, her voice a bit unsteady. Taylor straightened up and looked at her, her head tilted to one side.

"You were really worried about me, weren't you?" she asked.

"Just a little," she lied. She forced a smile. "Okay, maybe a bit more than that."

Taylor just watched her for a moment, a strange look on her face. She finally took her coat off and hung it in the closet before going into the kitchen. Callie took a deep breath and tried in vain to calm her racing pulse. The thought of anything happening to Taylor scared her more than she thought it would. More than it *should*. Definitely more than she'd expected. After a few minutes, when Taylor didn't return, she got up and went to find her.

Callie hesitated when she saw her standing at the sink, her hands on the edge of the counter, and her head hung down. When she saw Taylor's shoulders hitch, she went and stood beside her. She wanted nothing more than to put her arm around her, to comfort her, but she was pretty sure that type of contact wouldn't be welcomed.

"Are you okay?" Callie asked softly, ducking her head in an attempt to meet Taylor's eyes. "Did she come back?"

"Yes, and no," Taylor answered. She lifted her head but was careful to look the other way. "Yes, I'm fine, and no, she didn't come back. It all just kind of caught up with me when I saw how worried you were."

"I'm sorry if I upset you."

"You didn't," Taylor assured her. Her hand twitched with the desire to reach out and touch Callie's face. The look in Callie's eyes told her it would be okay, but there was something stopping her. She shoved her hands in her pockets and leaned against the counter. "It just reminded me so much of Andrea."

"I hope that's a compliment." Callie smiled. "People never give me enough compliments. It's frustrating, really."

"I see what you're doing here." Taylor laughed, and she felt herself relax. She was surprised to realize it was the first time since Randy had escorted Sharon out of the bar.

"Am I that transparent?"

"Just a wee bit," she said.

"I'll have to work on it then."

They both stood there, watching each other and not moving. Taylor felt a change in the air between them, and she wondered if Callie felt it too. The longer they stood there, the stronger the desire became to touch her. When she was certain she couldn't hold back any longer, Callie broke their eye contact, and the moment was gone.

"I think I need to get some sleep," she said.

"Okay," Taylor answered, feeling a little lost with the connection gone. "Just let me get some sweatpants from my room, and you can sleep in there."

"Are you sure? I've managed all right on the couch the past two nights."

"I'm sure. I'll just be a minute."

Taylor hurried to her room and went straight into the bathroom to splash cold water on her face. What the hell was going on? Touching Callie, kissing her, was all she could think about. But it was so wrong. They hardly knew each other. Why in God's name did Callie have to be the first person she felt an attraction to since Andrea? She was convinced the universe was playing a colossal joke on her.

A noise from the kitchen woke Taylor up from a sound sleep. Her first thought was Sharon had somehow found her and broken into the house. She got up, wishing Blaze had stayed in the living room with her instead of following Callie to the bedroom. She made her way slowly toward the kitchen, trying her best to not make any noise. She noticed her hands were shaking just as she reached the door, and she heard Blaze's nails on the floor.

"Good boy," she heard Callie say quietly. "Let's go back to bed before we wake your mom up."

"Too late," Taylor said, causing Callie to jump.

"Jesus Christ, you scared the hell out of me."

"I could say the same." Taylor walked to the fridge and got a bottle of water. She held one out to Callie before grabbing a second one for herself.

"Blaze decided he needed to go out, and he was very adamant about it. I tried really hard to be quiet, but you were snoring so loud, I didn't think you'd hear us." Callie leaned against the counter, and Taylor followed suit, the fact they were in this exact position earlier not escaping her notice. "Sorry we woke you up."

"I don't snore," Taylor said defiantly.

"I beg to differ," Callie said with a smile. "I think you could rival Blaze in that department."

She said nothing in response because the pull she'd felt earlier was there again, and Taylor was tired of fighting it. The moonlight coming through the window was enough to see by, and the way the light illuminated Callie's eyes was mesmerizing.

"I don't snore," Taylor said again, her voice little more than a whisper. She needed a distraction, so she looked at Callie's arm, still in its sling. "How's your shoulder?"

"It hurts, but not anywhere near as bad as it did. I'm healing."

"Good." Taylor took a drink of her water before setting the bottle on the counter next to her. Before she could think twice about what she was doing, she took a step toward Callie. The kitchen was small, so this succeeded in putting her only a couple of feet away.

"Taylor," Callie said, her eyes shifting to Taylor's lips for just a fraction of a second. Taylor could see her breathing was almost as quick as her own, which only emboldened her.

She reached out and tucked a strand of hair behind Callie's ear. Callie's eyes closed momentarily, and Taylor eliminated the remaining distance between them. When Callie looked at her again, she shook her head slowly.

"What are you doing?" Callie asked.

"I don't know," Taylor admitted. All rational thought was gone, and the only thing she wanted now was her lips on Callie's. And Callie's hands on her. Everywhere.

It was Callie who moved first, snaking her good arm around Taylor's waist and pulling her body against hers before gently pressing her lips to Taylor's. Taylor heard herself moan as she parted her lips to invite Callie in.

Callie deepened the kiss, obviously following Taylor's lead. The sensation of Callie's tongue sliding along hers was causing amazing things to happen, mostly between her legs. She put her arms around Callie's neck and tried to get even closer to her, but the kiss ended abruptly. Callie let out a hiss and pressed her forehead against Taylor's.

"Shit, I'm sorry," Taylor said when she realized she'd hurt Callie's shoulder.

"It's okay." Callie took a deep breath and leaned back slightly. When Taylor moved to pull away from her, the arm around her waist held her there. "Really, it's okay."

"No," Taylor said, shaking her head as she finally did back away from her. "None of this is okay. I don't know what I was thinking."

The hurt in Callie's eyes was evident, even in the small amount of light coming through the window. She hadn't wanted to hurt her, and honestly, she was ashamed of herself for initiating the kiss. She took another drink of her water before putting it back in the fridge.

"I'm sorry, Callie," she said again.

"Maybe we should talk about it?" Callie suggested before Taylor could leave the room.

Taylor didn't respond. She went straight to the couch and pulled the blanket over her head, facing the back of the couch. The embarrassment she felt at running away from it wasn't enough to dispel the realization that Callie kissing her had felt so right.

CHAPTER TWELVE

They managed to get through the next day without any awkward moments, and Callie was beginning to wonder if maybe she'd dreamt the kiss from the night before. When it came time for Taylor to leave for the bar, Callie slipped her shoes on and grabbed her jacket.

"Where are you going?" Taylor asked.

"I told you last night I was going to work with you."

"I didn't think you were serious."

"I don't always joke around," Callie said. She held the door open for her and they exchanged a look Callie couldn't quite identify, but she knew then without a doubt their kiss had really happened.

"Good to know, I guess," Taylor said, almost low enough for Callie to miss the comment.

They were silent for most of the ride to the bar, but right before Taylor turned into the lot on the side of the building, Callie decided to get a little more information on what had happened the night before.

"You said she got pushy. In what way?"

"She was coming on to me," Taylor said again as she pulled into a parking space and turned off the ignition before twisting in her seat to face Callie. "I told her I wasn't available, but it obviously didn't matter to her. At one point she grabbed my arm, and I twisted her wrist, which was when I told her to leave and then Randy showed her the way out."

"Randy?"

"Just a customer. I don't remember ever seeing him before, but he was very helpful."

Maybe it was just the cop instinct in her, but Callie wasn't sure she trusted this Randy character. For now she'd believe he had Taylor's best interest in mind, but she'd definitely keep an eye on him if he were to show up before the night was done.

"Okay, good," Callie said with a nod. "If she thinks you have a girlfriend—or boyfriend—we can use that. If she does come in tonight, I'm the reason you aren't available."

"No," Taylor said, putting the keys in her coat pocket and reaching for the door handle. "I won't do that."

Callie placed a hand gently on her forearm to stop her. It worked, but Taylor didn't turn to look at her.

"It's just for tonight, and only if she shows up." Callie let go of her and put her hand in her jacket pocket. "If pretending for one evening you're in love with me gets her to back off, isn't it worth it?"

Taylor said nothing, but after a few moments she finally nodded once and then got out of the car. Callie followed her into the bar, where Camille was getting things set up for when they opened in half an hour.

"Hey, Callie," she said with a wave. She pointed at her shoulder. "How does it feel?"

"Like I was shot," Callie answered with a grin. Taylor rolled her eyes and offered to take her jacket into the office. She gave it to her and then settled in at the bar.

"I knew I could count on you to say it." Camille laughed. When Taylor disappeared into her office, she set a cup of coffee in front of Callie and leaned on the bar. "I'm glad you're here tonight."

"I'm glad you made her call me last night. Thank you."

"I figured somebody needed to know what was happening in case it didn't end with Taylor throwing the woman out." Camille reached under the bar and pulled out an envelope she then placed on the bar and pushed toward Callie. "Which it obviously didn't."

"Where was this?" Callie resisted picking it up and looking at it more closely. There was only one word written on the envelope.

Taylor.

"It was taped onto the front door when I got here. Do you think I should give it to her?"

"You don't know for sure it's from her," Callie said, even though she knew they were both on the same wavelength in regards to who it came from. "How does she know her name?"

Camille winced slightly and looked away from her. "I think it was my fault. I called her name to get her attention so I could let her know I was going in the back for some ice. I'm sorry."

"Don't be sorry. You didn't know it was going to turn into anything. It still might not." Callie shrugged with her good arm and took a sip of her coffee. She wished she was sure of what she was saying, but her gut told her this wasn't a simple apology.

"Right," Camille said with a snort. She turned to make sure she had enough liquor for opening on a Saturday night. "So, will you give it to her?"

"Sure." Callie finally picked it up, and when she was about to get off her bar stool and take it to Taylor in the office, Taylor walked out with the cash for the register to start the night with.

"It's still a holiday weekend, so I'm not expecting an overly busy night," she told Camille, her back to Callie.

"I hate the slow nights," Camille replied. "Time seems to drag."

"Taylor?" Callie said. When she turned to face Callie, Callie looked down before holding the envelope out to her.

"What's this?" Taylor took it, and if Callie hadn't been so worried about what was in the envelope, she'd think the look of curiosity on Taylor's face was cute.

"It was on the door when I got here," Camille said.

Taylor folded it in half and stuffed it into the back pocket of the jeans she was wearing. Without a word, she turned and straightened the glasses on the back of the bar.

"Aren't you going to open it?" Callie asked, not even trying to hide her irritation.

"Not right now."

Callie let out a frustrated breath and took another sip of her coffee. This was infuriating. The contents of the envelope would no doubt tell them whether or not there was anything to worry about if it was indeed from Sharon. After a moment, Callie stood, went behind the bar, and took Taylor by the arm.

"What are you doing?" she asked as Callie led her toward the office.

"You're going to open it, and you're going to do it now." Callie knew her tone left no room for argument, and thankfully, Taylor seemed to realize it. She didn't say another word until they were in the office, door closed.

"I don't like being told what to do, especially in front of an employee." Taylor stood facing her, arms crossed over her chest.

"You can chastise me later, okay?" Callie never wished more than she did right then for the use of her right arm. She would have grabbed the envelope out of Taylor's back pocket and opened it herself. "Please, just open it."

Taylor stared at her for a minute before walking to the other side of her desk and sitting down. Callie stood watching her, one foot absently tapping the ground as she waited. She took a deep breath and closed her eyes for a moment.

"I don't think I can," she said. She was afraid of what it might contain. Obviously, Callie thought it was from Sharon, and Taylor had no reason to think it had been anyone else. What if it was a threat of some sort? She supposed there was no better time to open it than when there was a cop in the room with her.

She picked up a pen and slid it under the flap then slowly pulled it up so it ripped open across the top. There was a single sheet of paper inside, and when Taylor unfolded it, two tickets fell out. She glanced up at Callie, who looked to be as perplexed as she was. She saw they were tickets to the Rochester Americans. She looked at the paper they'd been folded inside of and found a note.

Taylor,
One of the guys I was with last night plays for the Amerks, and he wanted me to give you these as a thank you for the free round of drinks.
Randy

She handed it to Callie so she could read it. She laughed at Callie's confusion, and until then hadn't realized how relieved she was at finding out it wasn't from Sharon. She looked at the tickets, noting they were for the weekend before Christmas. The Americans, or, as they were more commonly referred to, the Amerks, were the local minor league hockey team of the Buffalo Sabres.

"This is the guy who helped you last night?" Callie asked.

"Yes." She stood and headed for the door. "He and his friends obviously noticed the pennant I have hanging behind the bar and assumed I was a fan."

"You aren't?" Callie seemed surprised. "Andrea liked to tell me how you guys always went to the games. She and I always went to the games together, so it kind of pissed me off a bit when she stopped going with me."

"We did always go," Taylor said with a nod. "But I haven't been since she died."

"Well then, we should go."

"*We* should?" Taylor couldn't stop the smile she felt tugging at the corner of her lips.

"I mean, you know, unless there's someone else you had in mind to take." Callie looked genuinely nervous now, and Taylor thought it was adorable.

Shit, where did that thought come from? She shook her head to dispel the notion, but Callie was still looking at her, apparently waiting for an answer.

"Maybe," Taylor said with a shrug. "It's a Saturday night, so I'm not sure I can be away from the bar, but I'll think about it."

Of course she was going to go, and there wasn't anyone she'd rather go with than Callie, but she wasn't about to tell her as much right now. Maybe it would be good to make Callie wonder about it for a while.

Taylor was considering letting Camille go home around eleven, but then she saw Sharon walk through the door. She glanced over at the spot at the end of the bar where Callie had been all night, but she wasn't there. Her panic must have been evident because Camille walked past her on her way to the cash register and bumped her shoulder.

"She went to the bathroom," she said with a grin Taylor thought looked more like a smirk. "Can't say I blame her after all the coffee she's put away tonight."

"She's here," Taylor said, following her to the register without looking over her shoulder at Sharon. "I'm going to the office for a minute."

She didn't wait for a response, but hurriedly made her way down the short hallway to the office. This was stupid. Camille being overprotective the night before, and then Callie insisting on coming here tonight was succeeding in making her much more nervous than she would have otherwise been about this entire situation. It wasn't like she hadn't dealt with people like Sharon before. Men and women both tried to ask her out, and she always handled it and moved on. Why should this time be any different?

She reached for the doorknob just as there was a knock, causing her to jump. She laughed quietly at herself before clearing her throat.

"Who is it?"

"Taylor, it's me."

Callie. Nothing to worry about. She unlocked the door and let her in. She could tell Callie knew Sharon was there, and Taylor wondered if Camille had gone into the bathroom to inform her. She wouldn't put it past her, and it would have been exactly what Quinn would have done.

"Did she say anything to you?"

"I came in here as soon as I saw her. I didn't give her a chance."

"Are you all right?"

"I'm fine, Callie. I was just about to go back out there when you knocked."

Callie nodded and they went back to the bar, Callie following closely behind her. Taylor glanced over her shoulder and gave her a slight nod before heading behind the bar, and Callie continued on to the seat she'd claimed before they even opened.

"Hey, beautiful," Sharon said with a wink. Taylor saw she already had a drink in front of her, so she simply smiled and moved on to help another customer. "Don't be like that, honey. I just want to talk."

"Honey?" Callie mouthed, one eyebrow raised in question when Taylor looked at her. Taylor shrugged and shook her head.

"Did you need something else?" Camille asked as she stopped in front of Sharon.

"I need the other bartender," Sharon said, the irritation obvious in her tone.

"She's busy with another customer. My name's Camille if you need anything."

Taylor saw Callie get off her bar stool and walk toward the pool table, which wasn't very far from where Sharon was sitting. She watched a couple who were playing, acting as though she wasn't interested in what was going on behind her, but Taylor knew she was close enough to hear everything.

"Taylor," Sharon called out. Taylor braced herself before turning and walking over to her.

"Is there a problem?" she asked, trying to sound pleasant.

"Yeah, there is. I didn't get your number last night," Sharon said with a wink.

"I told you I'm not available." Taylor was trying to discern if she was drunk again without being obvious about it.

"Yeah, you did, but what does it mean exactly?"

"It means she has a girlfriend," Camille said, butting into the conversation.

Taylor cringed at the words, but hoped Sharon didn't notice. She was going to kill Callie if she'd discussed this with Camille. To Callie's credit, she was still facing away from them.

"It's okay, I don't mind being the other woman." Sharon winked again. Taylor wanted nothing more than to slug her.

"I told you I'm not available," Taylor said again. She was fighting to keep her voice steady. "I'm not interested in anything you have to offer."

"Oh, ouch," Sharon said with a short bark of laughter. "How can you possibly know that without experiencing what I'm offering?"

"Because with what I've already got, I couldn't possibly want anything from anyone else." Taylor saw Callie turn toward them out of the corner of her eye, but she refused to look her way. "I'm quite happy with what I have."

"Whatever you think you have with your so-called girlfriend, I could give you so much more, trust me." Sharon shot a confident smirk in her direction.

Callie walked toward the bar, and Camille lifted the section that opened so she could get to where Taylor stood. Without any hesitation, she slipped her arm around Taylor's waist and kissed her on the cheek, letting her lips linger a little longer than was necessary.

"This is Callie, my girlfriend," Taylor said, surprising herself by not faltering over the lie. "Callie, this is Sharon."

"Pleased to meet you," Callie said. "I'd offer a handshake, but as you can tell, I have a bum arm. And there's no way I'm letting go of her."

"Believe me, if you ever do let go of her, I'll be right there to pick up the slack," Sharon said but Taylor noticed she had no cutesy little winks or smirks for Callie. Instead, she sat there staring at the two of them for a moment, her face growing red with what Taylor was sure was anger and not embarrassment. She slammed down the rest of her drink before getting up and storming out of the place.

"Okay, that went well, don't you think?" Taylor asked, not really making any attempt to get away from Callie, whose arm was still encircling her waist. She glanced over at Camille. "Is she gone?"

"Yep."

"I'd say it went well if it succeeds in getting her to stay away," Callie said, still staying exactly where she was.

Taylor felt herself lean into her, although it was the last thing she really wanted to do. She finally forced herself to pull away from Callie on her own and went directly back to her office, wondering why it was her body was betraying her by not listening to her mind.

CHAPTER THIRTEEN

So, you really think she's going to leave me alone now?" Taylor asked as they walked into her house later the same night. She walked right to the back door and opened it so Blaze could run out and do his business. She got a couple of waters out of the fridge and tossed one to Callie. Taylor wasn't so sure about it herself. "She looked awfully pissed when she left."

"I think telling her you aren't available, and then allowing her to see your girlfriend will be enough to deter any further problems."

"I hope you're right."

After letting Blaze back in, they went into the living room and sat on the couch, Taylor noting the fact Callie was sitting way too close to her. After a few moments of sitting in silence that wasn't entirely uncomfortable, Callie reached for her hand, and Taylor didn't pull it away.

"I think we should talk about it," Callie said.

"About what?"

"Seriously? Last night? The kiss?"

Taylor reached for her bottle, trying hard to come up with a response, but she didn't think Callie would buy it if she tried to tell her she'd been sleepwalking and didn't remember any such thing taking place. She shrugged and blew out a breath.

"What about it?" Taylor finally asked. "It happened, and it isn't going to happen again. It was a moment of weakness. I'm sorry."

"For what?" Callie squeezed her hand gently, but Taylor did pull away from her then. Callie sighed. "It was a good kiss. No, actually, it was a phenomenal kiss."

"Phenomenal, huh?" Taylor summoned the courage to look at her despite the heat she felt in her cheeks. "Then it's too bad it won't be happening again."

"It's a damn shame," Callie said with a grin. "I'd be more than okay with it if it were to happen again."

"It won't."

"Why not?"

"Callie, please." Taylor stood, needing to put some distance between them. She was finding it difficult to keep her wits about her when Callie was sitting so close to her.

"What? We're both adults here, Taylor. We kissed. Why is it such a horrible thing?"

Jesus, it was far from horrible, but Taylor didn't feel comfortable voicing her opinion on it. Callie was seemingly able to set her body on fire with just a look, and Taylor didn't understand why. Neither of them had ever looked twice at the other before Callie had been shot. And that—Callie being shot—was why she really didn't want to start anything with her.

"We aren't looking for the same things, Callie. If I ever get involved again, I'm going to want it to be forever. You prefer being with a woman once or twice and then move on."

"You don't know what I want." Callie sounded hurt at Taylor's words, but Taylor wouldn't allow it to influence her. "For your information, the last time I was with anyone was before Quinn and Grace got together. And before that, I was in a relationship for three years. I was faithful, she wasn't. I was ready to settle down, and I still am."

"You're a cop. You risk your life every day."

"I do, but I'm careful, I swear," Callie said with a nod. She pointed to her shoulder. "This was an anomaly, Taylor. Yes, I did something stupid and should have waited for backup. And, honestly? Maybe I am a little reckless sometimes, but never when I was with Jan. Not when I had someone to come home to."

Part of Taylor wanted to believe what she was saying, but she wasn't about to risk her heart again. Not on someone who might never come home to her. It had almost killed her when Andrea died, and she wasn't about to set herself up for that kind of loss again.

"There hasn't been anyone since Andrea," she said before she could stop the words from tumbling out of her mouth. To her horror, she felt her eyes fill with tears. She decided she needed a good stiff drink. Callie didn't follow her when she walked into the kitchen, which she was grateful for. There was no stopping the tears from falling, but there was no good reason for Callie to witness it.

She poured some whiskey into a glass and drank it all in one gulp, even though it was considerably more than just a shot. She put more in the glass and stood there looking out the window above the sink until her tears stopped. Once again, she downed it all in one drink, and this time it didn't burn going down like it had the first time. She rinsed the glass out, put the bottle back into the cupboard above the refrigerator and made her way back out to the living room.

She sat on the other end of the couch so there was some room between them. She really needed to have more furniture. Perhaps a recliner or something. But then again, this was the first time the seating arrangements had posed a problem. Honestly, it was the first time she'd had company other than her parents.

"I didn't know," Callie said quietly. "I mean, I know you said you hadn't dated, but you haven't even kissed anyone since then?"

"No, not even a kiss," she answered. "Until last night."

"Shit." Callie rested her head on the back of the couch as she spoke. "Then I'm the one who should be sorry. I really had no idea."

"Don't be sorry. You're the only one I've even wanted to kiss since then." Taylor leaned forward, her elbows on her knees. "Yet you're exactly the type of person I swore I'd never get involved with again."

"Because of the risk factor?"

"Yes."

"On the bright side," Callie said, obviously trying to lighten the mood, "Quinn will be home tomorrow, I'll be out of your hair, and we can both get back to our regular lives."

Really? Callie being gone was the bright side? It was amazing to think she'd grown so used to having Callie in her house, and it had only been four days. The tightness in her chest at the thought of Callie leaving surprised her almost as much as her desire to kiss her again did.

"I'm going to go to bed," Callie said as she got to her feet.

Taylor didn't say anything. She was afraid she'd say something she'd end up regretting, and that wouldn't bode well for either of them. No matter how lonely she was certain she'd be, she knew Callie leaving the next day was for the best. Nothing good could possibly come from them living under the same roof any longer than they already had.

❖

Callie showered and managed to pack up her things one-handed before she gave a last look around Taylor's bedroom. It was a shame to think she'd likely never see it again. But, she admitted to herself, it was probably for the best. Her late best friend's wife should probably be off limits anyway. She closed the door to the room before making her way down the hall to the kitchen, smiling when she saw Taylor sitting at the table with a box from Dunkin' Donuts in front of her.

"As you know, I don't cook, so this is breakfast," she said with a smile that succeeded in doing strange things to Callie's insides. She wondered, not for the first time, if Taylor had any idea just how beautiful she was.

"Cops and donuts," Callie chuckled, setting her bag down near the front door. She wasn't sure when Quinn was going to get there, but she figured the least she could do was be ready when she did. "Those references never get old."

"I didn't even think about that," Taylor said, sounding as if she meant it. Only the slight upturn of her lips told Callie she was teasing.

"No, seriously, they never get old because I love donuts," Callie assured her with a grin of her own. "Especially when they come from Dunkin'."

"Two sugars." Taylor pushed a large coffee toward her just as Callie took a big bite of a glazed donut.

She removed the lid and took notice of the absence of cream. Callie felt inordinately pleased to know Taylor remembered how she took her coffee.

"Breakfast of champions," Callie said before grabbing another donut. "Thank you."

"You're welcome."

They ate in silence, and Callie was grateful because she didn't know what to say. The few days she'd spent with Taylor had been better than she'd thought they would be, and in spite of everything, she felt they'd started on the road to friendship.

Of course, Callie wanted more, but she wasn't going to push. It was obvious Taylor was still struggling with life after Andrea, and Callie decided it would be best to just give her the space she needed.

They spent the day watching movies in comfortable silence, but when the doorbell rang around five in the afternoon, Callie breathed a sigh of relief. Taylor opened the door and let Quinn inside.

"Thank you for keeping an eye on her," Callie heard her sister say before she walked out to the foyer to join them. "I hope she wasn't too much of a pain in the ass."

"Gee, thanks, Quinn," Callie said.

"It was no trouble," Taylor assured her with a small smile directed toward Callie.

"Do I owe you anything?" Quinn asked, no doubt to rile Callie up, which she succeeded in doing.

"Damn it, Quinn, I have my own money, you know," Callie said. She picked up her bag with her good arm and headed for the door. She stopped and turned to Taylor before walking out. "Thank you again. And if I don't see you before, Merry Christmas."

"What are you talking about?" Taylor asked, looking confused. "We have a hockey game to go to on the seventeenth."

"Yeah?" Callie smiled. When Taylor nodded, Callie felt a relief she'd never experienced before. She was inordinately happy to know Taylor wanted to see her again. "Okay then. You have my number. Let me know the details." She gave her a quick one-armed hug and spoke quietly in her ear. "And call me if Sharon comes back."

Callie walked out the door feeling better than she had since the night they kissed.

Chapter Fourteen

Two weeks later, Callie was in physical therapy, her stitches gone, and she was back at work on desk duty until at least after Christmas. She'd stayed with Quinn and Grace for a few days until she was able to use her arm again, and she'd deftly avoided any conversations about Taylor, but at Sunday brunch less than a week before her date to go to the hockey game with Taylor, it seemed Quinn, Grace, and her mother all decided it was time for her to talk.

"You still think Taylor hates you?" Quinn asked as they all settled in to eat.

"I think I might be wearing her down." Callie grinned. She'd started going to the bar at least a couple of nights a week, and Taylor often sat and talked with her for at least a few minutes whenever she was there. Callie knew it hadn't escaped Quinn's notice, and she was surprised it had taken this long for her to say something about it.

"Just be careful," Quinn said.

"Excuse me?" Callie met her eyes before looking first at Grace, and then her mother, who both were intensely focused on their food.

"I'm just saying." Quinn shrugged and set her fork down. "She's not the kind of woman you can sleep with and then walk away from. She's not over Andrea yet."

"Shut up, Quinn," Callie said, fighting the irritation she felt bubbling up inside her.

"You have a date with her on Saturday, right?" Grace asked.

"It's not a date," Callie said, pushing her plate away. She'd lost her appetite thanks to this conversation. Despite her proclamation about it not being a date, she knew that was how she'd been looking at it. Taylor didn't have to take her, but she'd offered. The anxiety of not knowing if Taylor was viewing it as a date was adding to the annoyance she was feeling at this unwelcome conversation.

"Are you sure about that?" her mother asked.

"Yes, I am. Someone gave her the tickets, I happened to be there when she got them, and she offered to let me go along with her. It's not a date."

They ate in silence for a few minutes, but Callie could tell there was something more Quinn wanted to say. She kept glancing at her, but then she'd shake her head slightly and concentrate on her food again. It was driving Callie nuts. She finally dropped her fork on her plate and pushed her chair back from the table,

"What?" she asked Quinn.

"What?" Quinn asked, sounding defensive.

"Just spit it out for God's sake." Callie resisted the urge to stand and tower over her big sister. Instead, she remained seated and stared at Quinn. "There's obviously something on your mind, so just say it."

Quinn glanced at Grace and then their mother before putting her own fork down and wiping the corner of her mouth with the napkin she then placed on the table next to her plate. She pushed her chair back and mirrored Callie's pose.

"There was a woman at the bar last night who said I looked a lot like Taylor's girlfriend." Quinn arched an eyebrow. "You're the only person I know who I look like."

Okay, Callie had not been expecting that. Her first thought was to be pissed because Sharon was there again, but she took a deep breath and let it out slowly through her nose in an attempt to calm herself.

"Did she say anything else?"

"Are you kidding me?" Quinn asked. "That isn't enough?"

"Did you tell Taylor about it?"

Quinn just stared at her, and Callie knew she was growing impatient. If Taylor hadn't explained to Quinn what happened, then was it really her place to divulge the information? Or had Quinn not said anything to her about it? Callie was reluctant to offer up too many details without first knowing how much Quinn knew.

"Will you just answer me, please?" Callie asked in a normal tone, which she hoped would signal to Quinn this was something serious. "You didn't tell her Taylor doesn't have a girlfriend, did you?"

"Callie, what the hell's going on?" Quinn asked, sounding concerned. "I went along with it. I figured if Taylor wanted this woman to think she had a girlfriend, then there must be a good reason. Is it true? Are you two seeing each other?"

"No, we aren't." Callie risked a look in Grace's direction and wasn't surprised to find she and their mother both were watching this exchange with rapt interest. Callie sighed. She was going to have to give Quinn something.

"This woman—Sharon—first showed up there the night after Thanksgiving, and she was coming on to Taylor. I decided to go to the bar with her on Saturday. Sharon showed up again, and I pretended to be Taylor's girlfriend to get her to back off." Callie moved her chair closer to the table then and picked up her fork again. "Why didn't you ask Taylor about it?"

"She'd already gone home for the night. I didn't think it was worth calling her about when I knew I'd be seeing you this morning. Is this something we need to worry about?"

"I don't know," Callie replied. She wished to God she did know because she felt the need to protect Taylor, and that scared the hell out of her.

❖

Taylor was surprised to find Quinn on her doorstep when she returned from the grocery store. She gathered her keys and her phone before heading up to the porch. The food would be fine in the car for a bit since it was barely above freezing outside.

"Hey, Quinn," she said as she gave her a quick hug. "What brings you here?"

"Nothing much," Quinn answered with a shrug. "I just wanted to talk about something I learned from Callie this morning at brunch."

Taylor held her breath as she unlocked the door and motioned for her to go on in ahead of her. She'd fought with herself over whether to tell Quinn about Sharon, but it had begun to look as though she wasn't going to come back to the bar. Taylor figured that was what this had to be about because there's no way Callie would have told her about the kiss, right? God, how mortifying would that be?

"Why didn't you tell me about Sharon?" Quinn asked when they were seated at the kitchen table, each with a beer in front of them. Quinn looked hurt, but Taylor couldn't concentrate on someone else's feelings right now. All she'd been able to think about lately was Callie, and it unnerved her a bit, to say the least.

"I didn't purposely not tell you about her; it just never came up. I hadn't seen her in a couple of weeks, and I assumed it was over." Taylor took a drink of her beer but never broke eye contact with Quinn. "I guess I was wrong?"

"She came in last night after you went home."

"What did she say?"

"She said I looked a lot like your girlfriend." When Taylor didn't say anything in response, mostly because she hadn't a clue *what* to say since she wasn't sure how much information Callie had divulged, Quinn went on. "I told her it was probably my sister, Callie. What's going on, Taylor?"

Taylor hesitated for only a fraction of a second before telling her everything. There was no need to hold anything back from her. Except for the kiss, which was something she wanted to keep just for herself. Especially if nothing ever came from it. When she was done with the story, she felt exhausted.

"Wow, so Callie kind of came to your rescue."

"I don't need anyone to come to my rescue," Taylor assured her.

"No, I know, but Callie thinks you hate her."

"Yeah, we talked about that." Taylor smiled but then turned serious when she saw the look of concern on Quinn's face. "It's fine. We're good now."

"Cool," Quinn said, sounding skeptical. "You have a date with her this weekend."

Taylor had been taking another swig of her beer when those words were thrown out there, and she almost spit it all over Quinn. Instead, she managed to keep it in her mouth, but she began to choke on it. She waved Quinn off when she started to stand, and when she finally regained her composure, she shook her head.

"A date? Is that what Callie said?"

"No, she denied it." Quinn grinned. "I just wanted to find out if you thought it was a date. I think I got my answer."

They talked for a while longer, and when Quinn left, Taylor had the strange urge to call Callie. She wanted to hear her voice. She didn't understand why she felt so drawn to her seemingly out of the blue, and again, it was unnerving. She put the groceries away, left her phone on the kitchen counter intentionally so she wouldn't be tempted to call Callie, and went to the living room where she spent the rest of the evening watching television.

And thinking about Saturday night.

Which really made no sense to her. She'd actually felt disappointment when Quinn said Callie denied the hockey game they were going to was a date. After her admission that there'd been no one since Andrea's death, it was obvious Callie was backing off. Giving her room, so to speak. And for some reason, Taylor wasn't entirely happy about it.

"God, how much more wishy-washy can I be?" she said out loud. Blaze got up from where he was sleeping on the floor in front of the couch and whined softly. "Why does she have this effect on me, boy? She's a cop. I cannot get involved with a cop. Not to mention, she was your mommy's best friend."

Blaze rested his head on her thigh, and she absently rubbed his ears while trying to not think about Callie.

"I am so screwed."

CHAPTER FIFTEEN

Callie was trying her best to sleep on Wednesday night, three nights before they were supposed to go to the hockey game. She hadn't gone back to the bar since Quinn told her Sharon had shown up there again. She'd made Quinn promise to call her if she did, and she trusted Taylor would have let her know if she wanted Callie's help with her on a night Quinn was off.

She couldn't sleep. It was almost eleven, and she'd been trying for two hours. She finally threw the covers off and decided to walk the few blocks to the bar. Maybe a beer or two would help her to sleep.

When she walked in, Taylor was behind the bar, and she was talking to a customer. Taylor glanced over her shoulder and waved at her, causing Callie to smile. It seemed Taylor was always pleased to see her lately, which was a good dose of happiness for her, usually at the end of a long, boring day of desk duty. She walked over to sit by the man Taylor was talking to.

"Callie, this is Randy, the guy whose friend gave us the tickets to the game on Saturday," Taylor told her as she filled a pint from the tap and set it in front of her.

"It's nice to finally meet you, Randy," she said, shaking his outstretched hand. "I've heard a lot about you."

"I could say the same about you," he answered. "We're kindred spirits, in a way."

"How so?"

"I'm a cop too," he said. He puffed his chest out, then laughed. "Brockport's finest."

"Good to know," she said with a nod, feeling infinitely better knowing he was one of the good guys, and not a friend of Sharon's. He was a big guy, the kind you'd have to think twice about messing with. He was muscular, but not in a professional body builder sort of way.

"Want to play a game of pool?" he asked.

"Normally, I would, but I'm still recovering from a gunshot wound to the shoulder." She probably could play, and her physical therapist would no doubt be happy if she did, but she really just wanted to sit there and watch Taylor.

"Yeah, I read about it in the paper. Tough break, but at least you guys caught the bastard," he said. "Your first time taking a bullet?"

"First, and I hope the last time," she said with a grin. "I don't really recommend it to anyone."

"I'll keep that in mind." He chuckled and finished what was left of his beer. He frowned as he looked past Callie, which caused her to follow his line of sight.

Sharon. *Damn it.*

"Is she in here a lot?" Randy asked.

"More than Taylor would like her to be," Callie answered.

"Taylor told me you were pretending to be her girlfriend. I guess that isn't working so well, huh?"

"I think this woman just won't take no for an answer."

"She'll give up eventually," Randy said as he stood. "They usually do. She'll find someone else to fixate on, and then Taylor won't have to worry about her anymore."

"I hope you're right," Callie said, but she wasn't so sure. The stab of jealousy she felt when Sharon was watching Taylor made absolutely no sense. Taylor wasn't hers, but even if she was, she knew Taylor would never be interested in Sharon. Maybe what she was feeling was longing? Yeah, she'd go with that for now. Much easier to deal with than jealousy.

"I'm heading out. Taylor has my number if you need any help, okay?" Randy asked.

"Thanks, man," Callie said, shaking his hand again. "It was good talking to you."

He waved to Taylor as he left the bar, and Callie kept her eyes on Taylor, refusing to even acknowledge Sharon. She watched while Taylor got her a drink, and then while Sharon tried to chat her up. It was obvious to Callie that Taylor just wanted to get away from her, and when she finally did, she came right to Callie.

"My God, this woman is infuriating," she said, taking Randy's empty glass and setting it in the sink. "She refuses to leave me alone."

"Is she still hitting on you?" Callie reached across the bar and took Taylor's hand, knowing Sharon was watching. She rubbed her thumb along the back of her hand, and kept eye contact, smiling. "Maybe we should kiss. Maybe that would make her think twice about coming on so strong."

"Are you hitting on me now too?" Taylor asked, but she smiled as well, no doubt for Sharon's benefit.

"No, I'm flirting, and you've never indicated to me you don't like it. On the other hand, you've told her more than once to leave you alone, and she won't. There's a big difference."

"Is she watching us?"

"She's always watching you," Callie said. "She can't seem to take her eyes off of you most of the time, which I can certainly understand. You're beautiful, Taylor."

Callie was surprised when Taylor leaned across the bar and grabbed the front of her shirt, pulling her forward and pressing their lips together. There was nothing noteworthy about it, in fact it was rather chaste, but it ignited something in Callie anyway. Of course, where Taylor was concerned, it didn't take much to ignite her.

"I know you can kiss better than that," Callie said when Taylor pulled back slightly.

"Stop flirting with me," Taylor said, but Callie saw the smile that contradicted her words.

"But you like it."

"Maybe."

"Maybe? I think the word you meant to say was yes."

"Maybe." Taylor released the grip on her shirt after another quick kiss and went to work washing the glasses in the sink.

"I can't help it," Callie said with a shrug. "Flirting comes naturally with you."

"You're persistent, I'll give you that." Taylor laughed.

Callie watched her as she walked away, hanging the clean glasses on the rack above the bar. When she disappeared to the back room where the kegs were stored, Callie risked a glance at Sharon and saw she was watching her intently, a scowl on her face. Callie concentrated on the beer in front of her, and saw out of the corner of her eye that Sharon was walking toward her.

"You're cute together," Sharon said, and she didn't sound happy about it.

"Thanks," Callie said with a smile.

"But you're an idiot if you think I believe you're a couple."

"I'm sorry?" Callie turned in her seat to face her.

"Come on, if you two were really together, you'd be much more affectionate with each other," Sharon said, leaning against the bar next to Callie.

"Maybe we save our affection for when we're home," Callie said. "I've never really been too fond of public displays."

"But she would be," Sharon smiled, "if she were with me."

"She's not with you though." Callie smiled, even though what she really wanted was to punch her squarely in the nose. "Just in case you didn't know."

"When I see something I want, I get it."

"You might want her, but I have her. I suggest you back off."

"Is that a threat?"

"Not at all," Callie said in a tone far calmer than what she was feeling. "But when I'm with someone I love, I can be very protective."

"Then it should be a fun game." Sharon grinned, but Callie could see no humor in it. It was clearly meant to intimidate. "And I never lose when I play. And I don't take no for an answer."

"I hate to break it to you, but you've already lost."

"We'll see. May the best woman win."

Callie was seething by the time Sharon turned and walked back to her seat. Confidence in a woman was usually an attractive trait, but where Sharon was concerned, it was simply sinister. Callie felt as though she needed a shower after the exchange.

"What's wrong?" Taylor asked when she was done with whatever she'd been doing in the back. Callie looked at her and then at Sharon. "Did she say something to you?"

"She thinks she can win you away from me," Callie said. "There's something seriously off about her, Taylor."

"Yeah, I've sensed it too. I wish I could ban her from ever coming in here again."

"You can refuse to serve her," Callie said.

"I have a feeling that would make everything much worse."

"You're probably right." Callie mentally shook herself. She was thinking way too much about Sharon, and she was tired of it. She smiled at Taylor. "What time should I pick you up on Saturday?"

"I don't know. Do you want to have dinner first?"

"I'd love to."

"Well, the game starts at seven, so how about five?"

"Sounds good." Callie watched her as she walked away to get someone a drink, and wondered if she should have asked her if this was a date. God, how she wanted it to be. But she had the feeling a date was the furthest thing from Taylor's mind when it came to her.

Chapter Sixteen

"Y ou sure aren't acting like this isn't a date," Grace said while Callie was trying to find something to wear to the hockey game. Apparently, she and Quinn thought Callie needed help getting ready, so Grace had shown up at her apartment unexpectedly. "It's a freaking game, Cal. Jeans and a sweatshirt would be perfectly acceptable."

She knew that. She really did. But she wanted Taylor to notice her. She didn't want to just fit in with the rest of the people who would be in attendance. She finally decided on jeans and a green sweater.

"Okay, wow," Grace said when she walked out of the bathroom, fully dressed and ready to go. An entire hour before she was supposed to pick Taylor up. "That color looks fantastic on you."

"Yeah?" Callie asked, wondering if it was just a compliment to placate her, or if Grace was being honest. "You really think so?"

"Come sit with me." Grace patted the seat next to her on the edge of the bed.

She was living in the apartment above the bookstore Grace owned. Grace had lived there before moving in with Quinn when the two of them had finally admitted their feelings for each other. It had been the perfect solution for Callie, who had been staying in Quinn's spare room after returning from Atlanta when she'd left Jan. The only drawback to the apartment was the fact it was all one room, except for the bathroom. As a result, the only furniture in the place was the bed. She could probably fit a couch in the space too, but what would be the point? It wasn't like she did much entertaining.

Callie sat down and let out a breath, which caused Grace to chuckle. Callie looked at her and saw she had something she wanted to say. She waited patiently for Grace to say whatever was on her mind.

"You're nervous," she finally said.

"I am not," Callie answered, her tone defensive. She shook her head and looked at her feet. She was incredibly nervous, if she was being honest, and she knew Grace could tell. Grace knew her and Quinn both better than they knew themselves, it seemed. She raised her hand, her thumb and forefinger less than an inch apart. "Okay, maybe a little."

"You really want this to be a date, don't you?"

"Would that be a bad thing?" Callie picked at a fuzz ball on her sweater and didn't look up. "You know, if it *was* a date?"

"Oh, sweetie," Grace said as she put an arm around her shoulders and pulled her closer. "I don't think it would be a bad thing at all. In fact, despite what Quinn thinks, I believe it's way past time for Taylor to start dating again."

"She thinks I don't want a relationship."

"She told you that?"

"Yeah. And Quinn obviously thinks the same thing." Callie pulled away to look at Grace, knowing she was about to defend Quinn. "You heard her last Sunday. She told me to be careful with her. She warned me Taylor wasn't over Andrea yet. She thinks I'm going to break Taylor's heart."

"Are you?"

"What? No, I wouldn't do that." She stood and went to get a bottle of water, but mostly she just needed some space. She twisted the cap off and leaned against the fridge.

"But she has the power to break yours, doesn't she?"

Callie snorted. "Wouldn't that throw Quinn for a loop?" she said.

"Don't worry about Quinn, okay? I'll talk to her about this, and she'll get over whatever reservations she has." Grace watched her for a moment, and Callie looked everywhere but at her. "So, do you want a relationship?"

"When I left Jan, I thought the last thing I needed was another girlfriend. Someone who would make demands on my time, and expect me to do whatever they wanted to do, whenever they wanted to do it." Callie began picking absently at the label on her bottle before setting it down on the counter. "I figured every relationship was like the one I had with Jan. But I've watched you and Quinn together, and I see it can be a wonderful thing to have someone to come home to every night. To love you. To be on your side no matter what."

She met Grace's eyes, and damned if she didn't feel like she was going to cry. Crying was definitely not something she planned on doing tonight. She looked at the ceiling so she wouldn't have to see the love and understanding in Grace's eyes.

"God damn it, Grace, I want that," she said around the lump in her throat. "And I want it to be with Taylor."

"Whoa there, you're moving a little fast, don't you think?" Grace's skepticism was obvious, and Callie met her gaze as she shook her head.

"No, it isn't. Not really." Callie made her way back to the bed and sat down next to her again. "I mean, if you think about it, I've known Taylor since Quinn started working for her, and that was over fifteen years ago. I actually knew her before Andrea did. Granted, for the vast majority of the time we were nothing more than acquaintances."

"But you hardly know her."

"I know this is going to sound crazy," Callie said before she took a deep breath and went on because she knew if she didn't just say it now, she never would. "When she and Andrea started seeing each other, I was jealous."

"Because you loved Andrea?"

"God, no, she and I were too much alike," Callie said with a laugh. "That would have never worked out, and we never even attempted it. We were better as friends. I was jealous because I'd always had a crush on Taylor. I hated how they were so perfect together. Andrea told me so much about Taylor, I felt like I knew her. I made the mistake of telling her she was lucky she'd married Taylor because otherwise I'd steal her away. I never spent much time with the two of them when they were dating because I didn't want to see them so in love. Then, after that, Andrea told me Taylor didn't like me because I was so reckless and she thought for sure I'd end up making Andrea take risks she shouldn't. I believed what she said because I had no reason to think she would lie to me. But Taylor said she never told Andrea anything of the sort. I think Andrea just wanted me to stay away from Taylor because I was attracted to her."

"Has discovering this made you think less of Andrea?" Grace was holding her hand, and Callie was a bit mortified to realize she was indeed crying.

"No, it hasn't," Callie answered, wiping the tears from her cheeks. "Maybe it should, I don't know. But she was my best friend. I would have done anything for her. If I could have run into that building to save her, I wouldn't have hesitated. I think at some point I realized Andrea had very little self-confidence, even though she managed to hide it very well. I can't think less of her because she worried she wouldn't be enough to keep Taylor happy."

"So, Taylor does like you?" Grace asked, sounding a little tentative.

"Yes. I mean, I think so. We kissed," Callie said, and then wished she could turn back time and stop herself from saying it out loud. "If you tell Quinn, you know I might have to kill you, right? I'm a cop. I could cover it up if I needed to."

"I won't tell Quinn," Grace assured her with a slight chuckle. "Does Taylor have any idea how you feel about her?"

"Are you crazy? She knows I wouldn't mind if we kissed again, but it probably isn't going to happen."

"Why not?"

"She told me…" Callie let her voice trail off, silently thanking whoever might have been responsible for her stopping what she was about to say. It was not her place to say Taylor hadn't been with anyone since Andrea died. She shook her head.

"What did she tell you?"

"Nothing," Callie said. "It doesn't matter. Just suffice it to say this is not a date, and I'm just hoping Taylor and I can at least be friends."

"You'll tell me some day," Grace said with a finger to her ribs. "You know damn well you will, right?"

"I have no doubt." Callie smiled and grabbed a tissue to dry her eyes. "I'm smart enough to realize when Grace wants to know something, she ends up knowing it, no matter what."

"Just as long as you understand that, everything will be fine." Grace winked at her before glancing at the clock on the bedside table. "You'd better get going if you want to be on time."

"Oh, shit, I didn't realize we'd been talking so long."

"You know you can come to me anytime, right? If you need to talk?"

"I do." Callie stood and held a hand out to Grace to pull her to her feet, then Grace wrapped her arms around Callie's neck and held her close.

"And if Taylor can't see what an awesome person you are, then it's her loss," she said into Callie's ear before squeezing her briefly, planting a kiss on her cheek, and finally releasing her.

Callie stood there for a couple of minutes after Grace walked out the door, wondering if there might ever be a time when Taylor would see what an awesome person she was. *Not if you're late picking her up, she won't.* She grabbed her wallet and her phone and rushed out the door. If she was lucky, she'd get there right on time.

Exactly fifteen minutes later, Callie was standing on Taylor's front porch, wiping her sweaty palms on the legs of her jeans and wondering what the hell was wrong with her. She felt like she was fifteen years old and about to meet her date's parents. *Not a date, not a date, not a date.*

She kept repeating it over and over in her mind as she rang the bell and waited nervously for the door to open. When it did, all she could do was stare. Taylor was dressed similar to her, with jeans and a sweater. The only difference was where Callie's sweater was a bit baggy, Taylor's hugged her in all the right places.

"Wow," she managed after her eyes had gone all the way from Taylor's toes to finally meet her eyes, after a short detour around the chest area. She smiled. "You look great."

"You clean up pretty well yourself," Taylor said, a slight blush covering her neck and her cheeks. "I'm so used to seeing you in sweats, or dressed for work."

"Or topless," Callie said with a wink. "Don't forget topless."

"So that's how this night is going to be?" Taylor stepped out onto the porch and pulled the door shut behind her,

God, yes, if I have anything to say about it.

Chapter Seventeen

Red Lobster was Taylor's favorite restaurant, so she was happy when Callie suggested it for dinner before the hockey game. In fact, Callie had even called ahead and left her name so they wouldn't have to wait so long for a table.

After a short ten-minute wait, she found herself following the hostess—and Callie—to their table. She almost tripped over a chair because she was so busy watching the view in front of her. Callie turned to see if she was okay, and Taylor felt her face heat in embarrassment. Once seated, the hostess gave them their menus and left.

"You were watching my ass," Callie said with a smirk.

"I was not," Taylor lied.

"It's okay, you know. I don't have a problem with a gorgeous woman lusting after my ass." Callie raised her menu so Taylor couldn't see her face.

"I was not lusting after your ass, or anything else about you," Taylor said again, at a loss for what else to say. She too raised her menu, but after a moment of looking at it, and not really seeing any of it, she set it down on the table again. "Has anyone ever told you you have a huge ego?"

"A time or two," Callie answered with a shrug.

"You are so infuriating." Callie sat back in her seat. "I was *not* staring at your ass."

"Staring? Who said staring? I think you just gave yourself away." Callie chuckled. "So you weren't just watching my ass, you were *staring* at it. And actually, you never answered my question from the first day I was at your house. Do you like the view?"

"Keep this up and I might start to hate you."

"But I'm charming. You said so yourself."

"Hello, can I get you ladies something to drink?" the server asked with a smile as she stood next to their table.

They ordered their drinks, then both went back to their menus, Taylor hoping Callie would change the subject and not continue along the same tack. Unfortunately, she wasn't so lucky. Callie reached across the table and took her hand. Taylor was too surprised to pull it back immediately which gave Callie the time she needed to get a better grip so she couldn't pull away.

"What are you doing?" Taylor asked.

"Sharon told me the other night she doesn't believe we're a couple because we aren't very affectionate with each other," Callie said, her thumb rubbing lightly against the back of Taylor's hand. "I'm practicing. Besides, she could be here for all we know."

Taylor started to pull away, but she knew Callie could be right. She resisted looking around the restaurant to see if they were being watched. It occurred to her she liked Callie holding her hand, and the flutter in her chest and belly wasn't entirely unwelcomed, even though it wasn't something she'd experienced in quite a long time.

"Just admit you like holding my hand."

"I don't have a problem admitting it," Callie assured her with a grin that caused more fluttering. Taylor really liked being on the receiving end of that grin. "Do you?"

"I never said I liked it."

"But you do, or else you would have pulled away."

"Whatever," Taylor said, rolling her eyes.

Thankfully, Callie had released her hand when the waitress brought their drinks. They ordered their meals without having really looked at the menu much, but Taylor had known exactly what she wanted before they got there. One of the perks of going to a favorite restaurant.

"I'd like to share an observation with you, but I don't want you to get mad," Callie said, suddenly serious.

"Okay," she said. Taylor wasn't sure she liked serious Callie. She worried about what she might be about to say. She tried to be patient while she waited for Callie to go on, and then Callie took a deep breath, leaning her forearms on the table.

"I told Andrea on your wedding day it was a good thing she was marrying you because otherwise I'd steal you away from her."

Taylor just stared at her, not having a clue as to how to respond. She sat there, waiting. It wasn't an observation, so Callie must be about to say more.

"Shortly after, she informed me you didn't like me. That you hated me, actually. She never invited me to your house again, and I never questioned it." Callie took a sip of her beer. "Until I'd been shot, and you told me you'd never said it."

"I'm still waiting for the observation," Taylor said, seriously wondering where this was going.

"I'm getting there," Callie assured her. "Andrea never really had much self-confidence when it came to women. I thought she'd overcome her insecurities with you, but now I'm wondering if she only told me what she did to keep me away from you. Like she thought I might really try to steal you away."

"Wow," Taylor said, finally pulling her hand away. "Your ego isn't just huge, it's monstrous."

"No, it's not my ego," Callie said, shaking her head. "I never would have tried to steal you away, it was just a joke I made in passing, but looking back at it now I think she might have taken it seriously."

"She would never have thought I'd prefer you over her," Taylor said, but she thought back to the time she'd told Andrea she found Callie attractive. It had been early in their relationship, and it hadn't occurred to her that Callie hardly ever spent time with the two of them together after she said it. Damn it, was it possible? Could Andrea really have been so insecure in her abilities to keep her happy? No, they'd talked about her insecurities, and Taylor was positive she'd successfully assured Andrea she was completely happy with her. But, she remembered, Andrea had told her the same thing. *Callie doesn't like you,* she'd said. Damn it, why was she just now recalling that?

"That's not even what I'm trying to say," Callie said, obviously becoming frustrated with the conversation she herself had started. "Never mind. Forget I even brought it up."

Taylor felt bad now. Callie was trying to get to the bottom of something that was bothering her about the woman who'd been her best friend, and Taylor was succeeding in making her feel bad for bringing it up in the first place. She sighed and decided to let her off the hook. She just hoped she wouldn't live to regret it.

"I'm sorry," she said, covering Callie's hand with her own. "Don't let this inflate your ego any further, but when she and I started dating, I told her I thought you were cute. So even though I never considered what you're saying, I have to admit you might be right."

She wasn't sure what kind of reaction she'd been expecting, but she was surprised when Callie pulled her hand away and looked everywhere in the restaurant except at her. She spent a lot of time studying the décor on the wall next to their booth.

Their meals came, and they proceeded in silence. Callie was pushing her food around on the plate and didn't eat much.

She'd lost her appetite. She felt gutted to think she may have caused Andrea to doubt herself any more than she already did. Andrea certainly hadn't deserved that, but she'd honestly thought she knew Callie was only joking. They'd literally just been married, for God's sake.

"Hey," Taylor said after a few minutes. Callie finally managed to meet her eyes. "Tell me what you're thinking."

"That I'm an ass," Callie replied.

"Well, yeah, that goes without saying."

Callie laughed in spite of herself. For a moment, she worried it might turn into a crying jag, but the moment passed rather quickly. Taylor was smiling too, and Callie felt like a weight had been lifted off her shoulders.

"Gee, thanks," Callie said.

"You said it, not me."

"You think I'm cute." Callie grinned. She shoved some shrimp in her mouth and pointed at her with her fork, loving the embarrassment making itself known in the blush on Taylor's cheeks.

"I did then," Taylor said with a shrug. "I never said I think it now. You were, what? Mid-twenties? A lot of women were cute back then."

"Uh-huh." Callie nodded. "Whatever you need to tell yourself."

"Andrea may not have had much self-confidence, but you have enough for the both of you, and then some."

They finished eating, mostly keeping topics fairly safe, with the bulk of the conversation being about Christmas and what kinds of family traditions they had. When Callie finally cleaned her plate, she sat back with a contented sigh.

"I want to thank you," she said. Taylor looked at her, one eyebrow raised in question.

"For what, exactly?"

"For making me laugh. For making me feel not so bad about things."

Taylor shrugged as though it was no big deal. "You have a nice laugh," she said. "You should do it more often."

"I'm paying," Callie said when Taylor tried to take the check.

"I can pay for myself," Taylor said, refusing to let go.

"I'm sure you can, but you're taking me to the hockey game. The least I can do is pay for dinner."

"You do recall the tickets were free, right?"

"So, what's your point?"

Taylor shrugged again and let go of the check. When the waitress came back with her change, they left the restaurant with plenty of time to get to the arena before the game started.

"Thank you for dinner," Taylor said.

"You're welcome." Callie took her hand and was relieved when Taylor didn't object. Maybe this could actually turn into a date before the night was over.

Chapter Eighteen

At some point during the second period of the game, Taylor realized she'd taken hold of Callie's hand. Her first instinct was to pull away, but she was surprised to realize she didn't really want to. It felt nice, and she'd gone way too long without any physical contact with another human being. Holding hands with Callie felt good. But even more, it felt right. Callie looked at her and smiled.

Her inner voice screamed at her, asking what the hell she thought she was doing. She wondered if she was sending some kind of signal to Callie, and worried she might be. Yet she felt absolutely no desire to disengage their hands, which were now resting quite comfortably on Callie's thigh.

When the Amerks scored with less than thirty seconds left in the period to go up by one, they stood and cheered along with everyone else in the arena. When they sat back down, Taylor was a little disappointed when Callie didn't reach for her hand again.

"You want anything from the concession stand?" Callie asked when the period was over. "I need something to drink."

"I'll go," Taylor offered.

"You sure?" Callie reached into her pocket for money, but Taylor stopped her before she could pull it out.

"I've got it." Taylor stood and looked down at her. "You can buy next time."

Taylor wondered where that had come from, especially when she noticed the goofy lopsided grin Callie gave her. Would there really be a next time? Taylor found herself hoping there might be, but she kept her expression as close to neutral as she could.

"Next time, huh?" She nodded once and got comfortable in her seat again. "I just want a Coke, and maybe some popcorn or something if that's okay."

"Be right back." Taylor made her way past the other people in the row to get out, and was so preoccupied with her thoughts of Callie, she almost ran right over a man walking down the steps. He gave her a dirty look but said nothing. "Sorry."

All day long she'd been wondering what tonight was. A date? Just a couple of friends hanging out at a hockey game? She wasn't sure when she started hoping it was the former, but it certainly seemed like a date. Callie picked her up, which meant she'd have to take her home too. The compliment about how she looked, and Callie opening doors for her added to the feeling of a date. Then there was the hand holding. And had she actually mentioned a next time?

There wasn't a whole lot about Callie not to like. She was gorgeous. She was funny. Charming. Sexy. She shook her head to try to dispel the last thought. When was the last time she'd had that thought about anyone other than Andrea? Taylor assumed she would have at least been uncomfortable at seeing someone in that light, but instead it simply gave her a warm feeling. All over. *All* over. The realization made her smile.

There wasn't much to cheer about in the third period, as the IceCaps tied it up. The Amerks won it in overtime though, so it was a good night for the home team. On the way to Callie's car, she reached for Taylor's hand, and Taylor didn't even flinch. She laced their fingers together and Callie squeezed gently.

"Is this okay?" Callie asked.

"Yes." Taylor got that warm feeling again and was thankful Callie had asked. She added thoughtful and caring to the growing list of *things to like about Callie*. Strangely, there was only one thing on the list of things *not* to like about Callie—her job. Was it something she'd be able to overlook? "It was a good game."

"It was," Callie agreed as she opened the car door for her. "You can't ask for much more than a win. And the fact it went to OT makes it even better."

There was very little conversation on the way back to her house, which only served to give Taylor time in her own head to wonder what might happen once they got there. A part of her wanted to invite Callie in for a drink, but she worried it might send the wrong message. She closed her eyes for a moment and barely managed to not scoff at the idea. What would be the wrong message, exactly? Taylor wanted Callie, and the thought scared, but at the same time excited her.

It had been so long since she'd even thought about sex. Her life was full, or so she believed. But obviously there was something missing if she was considering this. What could it hurt to have a night of fun? To just go with it. She was sure it was all Callie would be interested in, so that made it an even more appealing notion.

But then there was the other part, the part of her that worried she'd be making a huge mistake. She'd never been good at casual sex. Maybe it would be best to simply send Callie on her way after she dropped her off. Yes, that was what she had to do. Then there'd be no reason to second-guess what she'd done afterward. Satisfied with her decision, she resolved to thank Callie for a nice evening, and send her on her way.

When she pulled into the driveway, Callie put the car in park but didn't shut off the engine. Taylor breathed a sigh of relief that Callie wasn't expecting to be invited in.

"Thank you for taking me to the game," Callie said.

"You're welcome. I had a good time."

"Me too."

Taylor took a moment to look at her profile while Callie was staring through the windshield. She really was a beautiful woman. She reached for the door handle but then hesitated. She surprised herself by saying what had been on her mind the entire ride home.

"Would you like to come in for a glass of wine?"

Callie looked at her, the surprise evident in her eyes. Taylor wanted to kick herself for putting her thoughts to voice, but she forced a smile, and after a few seconds, Callie nodded once, then cut the engine.

Once inside, Taylor let Blaze out before grabbing a bottle of wine. She turned to Callie and held it up to her.

"Maybe I should have said I only have red wine," she said. "I hope it's okay."

"It's perfect," Callie assured her. Her palms were sweating again, and she resisted the urge to wipe them on her jeans. She watched Taylor open the bottle and pour some into two glasses, wondering what it meant that Taylor had invited her in. Her heart was racing, and she was more nervous than she'd been on her very first date with a woman. Taylor was important to her, and she didn't want to screw anything up with her. She took the glass Taylor offered her and followed her out to the living room. Just as they had for most of the time Callie was staying with her, they sat on opposite ends of the couch.

Callie let her eyes wander around the room, not knowing what to say. She wanted to know why she was there. Why Taylor had invited her in. But she couldn't ask those things. She was actually afraid she couldn't speak at all. She wanted to be sitting next to Taylor. Wanted to hold her hand, caress her face, to kiss her again. She took a sip of her wine and almost choked on it, her throat was so tight.

"Are you okay?" Taylor asked.

"Fine," she managed to say. "Just went down the wrong way."

"You seem nervous, but I would think after the time you spent here you wouldn't be."

"I told Grace we kissed." Callie winced as soon as the words were out there. She'd never intended to admit it, but she couldn't take it back now.

"What? Why would you tell her?"

"I'm sorry." Callie set her wineglass on the coffee table and turned in her seat to face Taylor. "Grace is one of my best friends. She promised me she wouldn't tell Quinn, if that's what you're worried about."

Taylor didn't say anything in response, but simply stared at her. She'd expected Taylor to be angry, but she didn't appear to be. She seemed calm, which for some reason worried Callie.

"It doesn't matter if she does tell her," Taylor finally said. She held Callie's gaze, and Callie felt her pulse quicken at the intensity of it. "It doesn't have to be a secret."

"Okay," Callie said slowly. She stayed in her seat while Taylor got up to let Blaze back inside. This was not what she'd expected to be talking about. The weather, the newest movies, the hockey game. Those were all relatively safe subjects. *The kiss* was not, in Callie's opinion. And those safe topics were exactly what they talked about over the next half hour. Callie looked at her watch and saw it was after eleven o'clock. She stood and smiled at Taylor. "It's getting late. I should probably go."

Callie could have sworn she saw disappointment flash in Taylor's beautiful brown eyes, but then she too stood, and walked Callie to the door. Once there, Callie slipped her coat on and turned to face Taylor. She was surprised to find her only a few inches away. She swallowed hard.

"I really did have a good time," Taylor said. Before Callie knew what was happening, Taylor had a palm pressed to her chest, right above her breasts, and she walked her backward until she hit the door. "I don't know what it is about you."

And then Taylor's lips were on hers, gently at first, but Callie let out a moan when she felt Taylor's tongue demanding entry. She parted her lips, allowing Taylor in. She felt goose bumps over her entire body at the feel of their tongues engaged in an erotic dance. Taylor's hands were on her hips, and they slowly moved up, under the hem of her sweater. Callie broke the kiss when she felt Taylor's hands on her skin, the touch igniting in her a fire she was worried she wouldn't be able to put out.

"Taylor," she whispered, their lips so close she could feel Taylor's ragged breath which matched her own. Without another word, she turned them around so it was Taylor against the door, and she let her coat fall to the floor before cupping Taylor's face and kissing her again. She groaned at the rush of excitement between her legs and knew she was instantly wet with arousal.

"Callie, wait," Taylor said, pushing her away half-heartedly. Callie forced herself to take a step back, her heart beating so hard she thought it might beat right out of her chest. "I'm sorry. I don't think I can do this."

"Okay," Callie said, doing her best to make Taylor understand it really was. "It's okay. I'm sorry too. I shouldn't have let it get so out of hand."

"It isn't your fault." Taylor moved away from the door and put some distance between them, which Callie immediately felt. "I thought I was ready for this, but clearly I'm not."

"It really is all right, Taylor," Callie said gently. She picked her coat up and put it back on. "I'm not going to lie and tell you I didn't enjoy it, but I understand. I won't ever push you into doing something you don't want to do, okay?"

Taylor nodded, and Callie pulled her into a hug. She kissed her temple and moved her mouth so it was close to Taylor's ear.

"Whatever you're feeling? It's okay. I would never judge you." Callie took a moment to breathe in the coconut scent of Taylor's shampoo and closed her eyes. She pulled back and waited for Taylor to make eye contact. "And I'm here if you ever need to talk."

"Thank you," Taylor said before hugging her again and pressing her lips to Callie's cheek. "For understanding. For being a friend when I didn't know I needed one."

"Is it okay if I come into the bar after work next week?" Callie braced herself, half expecting Taylor to ask her to stay away.

"You're welcome there anytime," Taylor assured her with a smile. Callie felt an odd fluttering in her stomach when Taylor's gaze moved to her lips for a split second.

"Good night, Taylor," she said, reaching for the doorknob. She knew she needed to leave before something happened they might both regret. She could tell Taylor was barely hanging on to her assertion about not being ready. And Callie really didn't want anything to happen between them if she wasn't completely ready for it. It would only end badly for them both.

"Good night." Taylor stood in the open doorway watching her until she pulled out of the driveway.

She stopped for the intersection at the end of the road and pulled her cell phone out. After looking at the text message she'd missed from about an hour earlier, she smiled and typed in a quick response to Grace.

On my way.

Chapter Nineteen

Grace was sitting at the end of the bar, probably nursing the beer sitting in front of her. Grace was a bit of a lightweight when it came to drinking, and it had become a running joke between the two of them and Quinn.

"Hey," Grace said when Callie made herself comfortable on the stool next to her. She bumped Callie playfully with her elbow. "How was the game?"

"Good." Callie nodded when Quinn held up an empty pint glass. She looked at Grace and smiled, remembering Taylor holding her hand at the game. "It was really good."

"Are we still talking about the game, or the company you were with?"

"Both."

"Cool. I assume she didn't ask you to stay the night, or you wouldn't be here, right?"

"Very astute." Callie chuckled and took a drink of her beer. She leaned closer to Grace. "There was kissing though."

"Really? Tell me more."

"I would say I'm not the type to kiss and tell, but I think I already did."

"There's that, and I've met you."

"Yeah." Callie nodded as she stared into her beer. She wanted to tell Grace, but even though Taylor said they didn't need to keep it a secret, she didn't want Quinn to know. She just didn't want to hear the warnings again about being careful with Taylor. After a few beats of silence, she turned her head toward Grace and smiled. "It was good."

"Good?" Grace wrinkled her nose and shook her head. "That's it?"

"Mind-blowing? Best kiss ever?" Callie laughed as Grace motioned for her to go on. "Knock my socks off good."

"Wow." Grace looked at her like she'd never seen her before.

"What?"

"I've just never heard you use any of those phrases before. It must have been some kiss."

"Oh, trust me, it was," Callie said with a nod. She shifted on the stool, her body reacting to the memory filling her mind of having Taylor pressed between her body and the front door. "I don't think I've ever fully appreciated how arousing being kissed could be until now."

"Why are you two talking about kissing?" Quinn asked as she stopped in front of them. She looked back and forth between them, an eyebrow quirked in question. "Are you trying to steal my girlfriend?"

"Please." Callie laughed before taking another drink, but never breaking eye contact with Quinn. "Think about what you just said. Do you really think I'd have to try?"

Callie pulled away quickly, but still not fast enough, when Quinn snapped a bar towel against the hand she had resting on the bar, and Grace laughed. Callie looked at her, trying to appear indignant.

"Nice," she said, nodding her head as she rubbed the back of her hand. "I'm glad you can take pleasure from my pain, you sadist."

"You've got to admit you deserved it, little sis," Quinn said, holding back laughter of her own.

"I'll admit to no such thing." Callie kept a straight face for about two seconds, which is when she started laughing too. "Damn it, that's going to leave a mark. You'll have to answer to Mom tomorrow, you know."

"I can handle Mom, Cal. And she'll probably agree you deserved it."

She wanted to deny it, but she knew Quinn was no doubt right. Quinn always had been her favorite. She just hoped right now Quinn would let the subject drop, but of course, she was never that lucky.

"So, why all the talk about kissing?" she asked as she leaned forward, her forearms resting on the bar.

"Don't you have customers to attend to?" Callie asked.

"Nope, everybody's good."

"Quinn," Grace said, and Callie saw her shake her head out of the corner of her eye. And she knew it would only fuel Quinn's quest for an answer.

Callie watched the two of them, wondering how the silent conversation thing worked because she'd never experienced it before. The moment it dawned on Quinn what they were talking about was almost comical, except she knew what was coming next.

"You kissed Taylor?"

"She kissed me, truth be told," Callie said with a shrug.

"I told you to be careful with her, Callie."

"Yeah, you did, and you know what? She's an adult. And I'm an adult too, in case it's escaped your notice." Callie drank again, and then looked at Quinn, daring her to start something. "What was I going to do, tell her oh, no, Taylor, we can't kiss because Quinn wouldn't like it?"

"You're an ass," Quinn said.

"Yeah? Look in the mirror because right now you're being a pretty big ass too."

"I swear to God, Callie, if you hurt her—"

"Really? I'm your sister, Quinn, just in case you forgot." Callie couldn't believe Quinn was acting this way. She did her best to keep her temper in check though because causing a scene in a public place had never been a high priority on her list of to-do items. "Shouldn't you be warning her about not hurting me?"

Quinn tossed the towel she was holding under the bar and walked away without another word. Callie stared at her for a moment until Grace tentatively touched her arm.

"Are you okay?"

"That went well, don't you think?" Callie asked with a forced smile. Grace looked truly worried, and Callie couldn't believe she was the one who was going to do the reassuring. "You know she and I argue like this all the time. We'll be fine as soon as she realizes she doesn't need to protect Taylor from big bad Callie Burke."

"I don't even know what to say, Callie."

"Don't say anything. Trust me, it'll be fine." Callie downed what remained of her beer before standing up and tossing a five-dollar bill on the bar. "I'll see you at brunch tomorrow."

Everything would have been perfectly okay if she hadn't turned around and ran right into Sharon, almost knocking her to the floor.

"Watch where you're going, dumbass," Sharon said as she jerked her arm out of Callie's grasp. Her demeanor did a complete one-eighty when she saw Callie's face. "Oh, it's you. Where's your girlfriend tonight?"

"That's really none of your business, is it?" Callie knew provoking her probably wasn't a good idea, but she just couldn't help herself.

"Bitch," Sharon said under her breath.

Callie so wanted to punch her. And she probably would have if she hadn't felt a twinge of pain in her shoulder when she made a fist and started to raise it. She felt Grace's hand grip her left bicep and she took a deep breath.

"Let it go," she heard Grace say with her mouth close to Callie's ear.

Callie willed herself to relax her taut muscles, and she tilted her head one way, then the other, thankful when she felt her neck crack, and some of the tension she felt dissipated. She took a deep breath and turned to Grace, leaning close so she didn't have to worry about Sharon hearing her.

"Can't I please just slug her once?"

Grace shook her head. "Not a good idea."

"You're no fun."

"That's not what you said when we were dating so many years ago." Grace smiled.

Callie couldn't help but laugh. She turned back around and saw Sharon still standing there, looking like she wanted a fight. Callie simply shook her head at her and walked out of the bar, half expecting her to follow. She actually felt a little let down when she didn't. She got in her car and pulled out her cell phone. Before she could think about it too much, she found Taylor's name and hit the call button.

"Hello." Taylor's voice sounded husky, like she'd been asleep.

"Hey. You weren't sleeping yet, were you?"

"Just dozing on the couch. Is something wrong?"

"No," Callie said, her eyes on the door to the bar. "I just wanted to give you a heads-up. Quinn knows we kissed."

There was silence from the other end of the line, and Callie pulled the phone away to see if they'd been disconnected. The call timer was still counting.

"Taylor?"

"It's okay," she finally said. Callie heard her urging Blaze to let her up. Taylor laughed softly. "I think he's not happy you left."

Callie didn't know what to say, so she said nothing. She simply waited for Taylor to say something else. She wanted Taylor to tell her she wasn't happy she'd left either, but didn't hold out much hope for a confession along those lines.

"I'll talk to Quinn about it tomorrow night at work."

"What are you doing tomorrow morning?" The words were out of her mouth before she even knew what she was saying.

"Why?" Taylor sounded skeptical, yet intrigued at the same time.

"We have brunch at my mother's every Sunday. Maybe you should come."

Silence again, but Callie took it as a good sign this time. The door to the bar opened, and Callie slumped down in her seat in case it was Sharon, but it was a couple of men. She closed her eyes.

"Never mind," she said when she assumed Taylor wasn't going to answer. "It was just a thought. You don't have to if you don't want to."

"What time?" Taylor asked.

"I can pick you up at ten?"

"I'll be ready."

When they hung up, Callie sat there for a moment trying to figure out what happened. She smiled. For a moment she considered going back inside and letting Quinn know Taylor would be there, but then decided it might be fun to surprise her.

CHAPTER TWENTY

Taylor pulled the door open at exactly ten o'clock the next morning, impressed that for the second day in a row, Callie was on time. Not early, not late, but right on time. Callie flashed her a grin that threatened to buckle her knees, but she somehow managed to stay upright. She took the Dunkin' Donuts coffee cup Callie held out for her and stepped aside to let her in.

She watched in silence as Callie got down on the floor and played with Blaze, which made him instantly happy. Taylor regretted she didn't play with him that way nearly as often as she should anymore. He wagged his tail and barked once as he got down to face her, his butt in the air and his tail moving faster than Taylor thought was possible. Taylor couldn't help but laugh at their antics.

"He likes you, you know," she said.

"That's good because I like him too." Callie rubbed his belly when Blaze flopped onto his back, panting, and tail still wagging. She stood and faced Taylor and her damned grin was back again. Was it possible Callie knew how she affected her?

"Should we get going?"

"We have time," Callie said, taking a seat on the couch. She patted the cushion next to her, and Taylor shook her head.

"You're in a good mood this morning," she said as she sat at the opposite end of the couch and turned her torso to face her.

"I'm trying because I think as soon as we show up, Quinn is going to ruin it."

"Why?"

"She wasn't too happy when she found out we kissed."

"It's none of her business," Taylor said. She set her cup down and tucked a lock of hair behind her ear that was suddenly bothering her. She knew Quinn looked out for her, and she appreciated it. But what was—or wasn't—happening between her and Callie wasn't her concern.

"I agree, but for some reason she doesn't see it that way." Callie looked at her, and Taylor couldn't find the strength to break the contact. Callie continued in a softer tone. "All she sees is me trying to get into your pants. Trying to take advantage of you."

"Is that what you're doing?" Taylor waited for an answer, trying her best to ignore the pulse between her legs as Callie continued to hold her gaze. How was it possible for Callie to cause such an immediate reaction simply by looking at her? She wasn't surprised when Callie scooted a little closer to her and took her hand.

"No."

Callie's single word, spoken with such sincerity, succeeded in making Taylor feel lighter than she had in ages. Had she really been so worried Callie was only after one thing, and when had she started to hope she wasn't? She reached out and brushed the backs of her fingers against Callie's cheek as her heart rate sped up. It was getting harder to take a breath.

"Jesus, Callie," she said, her voice strained. "How do you do this?"

"Do what?" To her credit, Callie hadn't moved, hadn't tried to lean in to kiss her. It was almost as though she knew it wasn't what Taylor needed right then.

"Make me feel. Make me want things I thought I'd never want again." Taylor shook her head in wonder. When Andrea died, she vowed to herself she'd never let anyone close again. And she'd been successful in keeping her promise for the past three and a half years. And then Callie had to come along, and make her feel alive again. She wanted to believe Andrea would be happy about it being Callie she was finally feeling this way about.

"I guess it's just my charisma," Callie said with a shrug. "I'm irresistible. What can I say?"

"And modest too." Taylor chuckled. "Don't forget modest."

"Who needs modesty when you have this level of magnetism?"

"Okay, now you're just being egotistical." Taylor laughed when Callie seemed to not have a comeback for that one. "We should go."

They stood, but Callie grabbed her hand when she started to walk toward the door. Taylor turned and faced her, instantly turned on by the look in Callie's eyes. She fought to not show it outwardly. Callie pulled her closer and placed her hands on her hips.

"You make me feel things too, Taylor," she said. "Things I've never felt before. I did use to live that life, wanting nothing more than to get into a woman's pants, but it isn't what I want anymore. Look, you know I'm interested, right?"

Taylor nodded, not trusting herself to speak at the moment. All she could think about was what Callie would feel like, what she smelled like, learning how she liked to be touched.

But what invaded her thoughts the most, was wondering how Callie's hands would feel on her skin.

"That isn't going to change, okay?" Callie ducked her head to meet her eyes when Taylor looked away. "I've felt this way since the first time I met you, so I can promise you it isn't going to change. But I'm not going to push you. If anything is ever going to happen between us, you need to be the one to initiate it. I will never try and get you to do something you don't want to do. Do you understand what I'm saying?"

Taylor felt herself nodding, but she searched Callie's eyes for any sign of deceit. Since the first time they met? How could that be? She'd known Callie before she ever met Andrea, and if it was true, why hadn't she ever said anything before?

"Let's go," Callie said, breaking their connection and heading for the door. Taylor had no choice but to follow, but her mind was a muddled mess.

She just hoped she'd be able to get a grip on her emotions before they got to Linda Burke's.

❖

They didn't talk on the way to brunch, and Taylor spent the time trying to understand what exactly had happened. It seemed as though there was a shift in the dynamic between them, and she wondered if Callie had felt it too. Thankfully, by the time Callie parked at her mother's apartment complex, she felt almost normal again.

"You're late," she heard Quinn call from the kitchen when they walked through the front door. Callie looked at her, and she seemed to be panicked.

"I'm sorry I didn't warn you before, but no one knows I'm bringing you here," Callie said quietly after stopping her from going any farther than the entryway. Taylor must have looked like she was going to bolt, God knows she wanted to, because Callie gripped her forearm and smiled. "It's okay, I promise. I just didn't think about letting them know."

"Thanks a lot for just tossing me into the fire," Taylor murmured just as Quinn rounded the corner. She smiled at her, but Quinn just looked confused. "Hi, Quinn."

Quinn stared for a moment, but then looked at Callie and reached for her arm.

"We need to talk," she said, not sounding happy.

"Your lack of manners are showing, Sis," Callie said as she pulled her arm away.

"Maybe I should go," Taylor said, feeling uncomfortable. She didn't necessarily feel unwanted, but it was obvious Quinn wasn't happy she was there.

"I'm sorry," Quinn said, seeming to realize she'd been rude. "You're more than welcome here, Taylor. Mom always tends to make enough food for twenty people. Grace is in the kitchen. I just need to talk to Callie for a minute."

They walked into the living room, and Taylor didn't even think about it—she followed them. She knew Quinn thought she'd effectively dismissed her, but she wouldn't be so easily pushed aside.

When Quinn turned toward Callie and realized she was still there with them, she started to say something to Taylor, but Taylor put a hand up and shook her head to stop her.

"I'm pretty sure whatever it is you have to talk to her about concerns me, so no, I'm not going to join Grace and your mother in the kitchen." She stood there waiting, arms crossed over her chest, and Callie smiled at her. It felt incredibly good to have Callie smile at her.

"Why did you let her kiss you?" Quinn asked after a beat of silence. Taylor smiled now because it seemed as though she was going to be the focus of Quinn's attention instead of Callie.

"I kissed her, actually. Well, last night I did. The first time—"

"The *first* time?" Quinn asked, her face beginning to turn a lovely shade of purple. "How many times has it happened?"

"I don't see how it's any of your business, Quinn," Taylor said, slowly shaking her head but remaining amazingly calm in the face of what felt like an interrogation.

"Did you fuck her too?" Quinn directed this pleasantness to Callie, whose face was steadily becoming more red by the second, but still not coming anywhere close to Quinn's attractive purple hue.

"Quinn Burke!"

They all turned to see Linda, Quinn and Callie's mother, standing in the entrance to the living room from the kitchen. Taylor glanced over her shoulder and was happy to see Quinn appeared properly scolded. She winked at Callie, who tried to hide her smile.

"I'm sorry, Mama," she said, sounding like a ten-year-old girl.

"In the kitchen now," Linda said, her voice sufficiently demanding. "All of you."

Quinn and Callie walked by her first, and when Taylor approached her, Linda put an arm around her and hugged her.

"It's so good to see you again, Taylor," she said with a warm smile. "I'm just sorry it had to be on a day when the two of them are acting like children."

"Who are you kidding, Linda?" Grace called over her shoulder. "These two always act like children. Hi, Taylor."

"Hello," Taylor said. "Unfortunately, I think they're acting this way because of me."

She took the seat at the table next to Callie, who was staring at Quinn seated on her other side. Taylor was just grateful she was sandwiched between Callie and Linda. Grace brought glasses filled with orange juice to everyone and took the seat on the other side of Quinn.

"That can't be true," Linda said with a pointed look at both of her daughters. "What caused you to ask such a vulgar question, Quinn?"

"My apologies," Quinn said quietly, but it was apparent she wasn't going to offer any further explanation.

"We kissed." Callie looked at her, a silent apology in her eyes. Taylor reached for her hand which was resting on the table. She intertwined their fingers and squeezed gently, hopefully conveying to her it was okay.

"Oh?" Linda asked, looking pleased. Her expression turned hard when she addressed Quinn again. "And that was what prompted your wildly inappropriate question?"

"They kissed twice," Quinn said.

"Damn it, Quinn," Taylor said, not able to be quiet any longer. "I know you want to protect me, but I'm an adult. I'm pretty sure Callie is too."

"That's debatable," Quinn interjected.

"I can take care of myself," Taylor said.

"Of course you can, dear," Linda said, looking at her hand still holding onto Callie's. "And I'm sure Quinn realizes that as well."

"I never knew you thought so little of me, Sis." Callie looked truly hurt, and Taylor felt the desire flare in her gut to hold her. To rush to her defense. "I'm not someone she needs to be protected from."

"I'm sorry," Quinn said with a sigh. "I guess I'm just assuming you went back to how you lived your life before Jan."

"Well, I haven't," Callie said. She looked like she was going to get up and leave, so Taylor gripped her hand a little harder to get her to stay. It seemed to work because Callie sat back in her chair and offered a small smile. She looked back at Quinn. "I want what you have."

Taylor was taken aback at the words, but she forced herself to not show any outward signs of her surprise. She'd been close to talking herself into having a night or two of fun with Callie, but knowing she wanted more than that changed everything, didn't it?

Chapter Twenty-one

Callie was quiet on the drive back to Taylor's house. She was still a little pissed at Quinn for thinking Taylor needed protection from her, even though they'd come to some kind of unspoken truce on the matter. The rest of the time at her mother's had been strained, and she knew Taylor had been almost as uncomfortable as she'd been.

She was a little overwhelmed by the depth of her feelings for Taylor, but then again, as she'd told Grace the day before, and Taylor herself that very morning, she'd been attracted to her for years. She just hadn't been able to explore the attraction on a deeper level before now. Spending those four days with Taylor after she'd been shot had brought the realization the attraction had become more than something physical. At least it had for her.

"Callie?"

She blinked and saw she was just turning into Taylor's driveway. How long had she been trying to get her attention, she wondered. It worried her to realize she didn't remember most of the drive from her mother's apartment.

"What?" she asked, knowing Taylor was waiting for an answer to some question she never heard. She turned the engine off and unclasped her seatbelt before recognizing her actions could be construed as her assuming she was going to be invited in.

"I asked if you were okay," she said, placing a hand tentatively on Callie's thigh. "Where were you just now?"

"I was right here with you." Callie flashed her a smile, but she could tell Taylor wasn't buying it. She really didn't want to have this conversation right now.

"Bullshit." Taylor pulled her hand back and looked out the window. She sighed audibly. "I was trying to ask you a question for more than a minute, and you were so lost in your own head you didn't even react to it."

"Look, Taylor—"

"Come inside with me," Taylor said quietly while not turning her head from the window beside her. "We should talk about some things."

Callie wanted to say no. She wanted it more than anything because she knew if they were sitting next to each other, talking about their feelings, she might not be able to stop herself from touching her. Kissing her. And she'd told her just a few short hours ago if anything was going to happen, it would be because Taylor wanted it.

"Please?"

Callie's breath hitched at the plea, spoken so softly she almost didn't hear it. Who was she kidding? She knew she would never be able to say no to Taylor. She'd do anything for her, and be happy while she was doing it because it would mean she'd be with her. Callie averted her eyes when Taylor finally turned her head to look at her.

"Please?" she said again, and Callie found herself nodding.

Once inside, Taylor grabbed a couple of beers and joined her on the couch. She sat close enough to Callie for their thighs to touch, and Callie put a hand on her leg before she could even think about what she was doing. She pulled it away quickly.

"I'm sorry."

"For what?" Taylor reached over and took her hand. She brought the hand up and pressed her lips to it before replacing it on her thigh. She kept her hand over it so Callie couldn't pull it away again. "I don't mind."

Callie looked at her, her pulse pounding in her ears so loudly she thought she must have heard her wrong. But the way Taylor was slowly rubbing her thumb against the back of her hand affirmed she hadn't. She swallowed hard.

"You are so beautiful," she heard herself say, and Taylor smiled shyly before looking down at their hands. "You have no idea what you do to me."

"Tell me what you were thinking so hard about in the car."

"You," she admitted, her voice barely more than a whisper.

"What about me?"

Callie let her head fall back against the couch, and Blaze chose that moment to jump up next to her. He lay with his front paws and his head in her lap. She used her free hand to scratch behind his ear as she spoke.

"I can't talk about this right now," she said.

"Why not?"

"It's embarrassing."

"Were you imagining me naked?"

Callie chuckled deep in her throat at the flirty tone Taylor used, but she made no move to look at her.

"No."

"Okay, then why don't you tell me why you ran out on your girlfriend?"

"I didn't run out on her," Callie said, sounding more defensive than she'd intended. "I'm pretty sure I told you she cheated on me, but she denied it. She did, however, tell me she was in love with someone else. I just left her before she had the chance to leave me."

"Oh."

It was understandable Taylor would be surprised by the fact she hadn't simply grown tired of being in a relationship and ran away when it got to be too much. It was how Callie had lived her life up until the point she met Jan. Hell, *relationship* wasn't even in her vocabulary before Jan. She knew in her head it was a logical conclusion, but it did little to ease the stab of pain in her heart to know Taylor thought so little of her.

"I see my reputation precedes me," Callie said, resisting the urge to rub her chest over her heart because the pain seemed to be so damned real.

"I jumped to a conclusion I never should have jumped to, Callie." Taylor gently gripped her chin and forced her to meet her eyes. She shook her head. "I'm sorry. I should have given you the benefit of the doubt, but you have to know why I leaped to that conclusion."

"I'm sure Andrea told you many stories about me to paint me in a less than flattering light. And you should probably know, most of those stories are no doubt true." Callie searched her eyes for some kind of understanding. "But I was younger. I wasn't ready to settle down. I met Jan, and I thought she was the one. I wanted her to be. Hell, I uprooted my life to follow her to Atlanta. It almost killed me when she admitted her love for another woman, but it didn't take me long to realize I loved the *idea* of forever more than I ever loved her."

Taylor released her chin, but let her fingers slowly move down her neck, causing Callie to shiver. She let her gaze drop to Callie's lips, and Callie let out a small moan.

"Jesus, Taylor," she said. "You're killing me here."

Taylor said nothing, but felt the overwhelming urge to feel Callie's body under her. Without giving any thought to what she was doing, Taylor gently pushed Blaze off Callie's lap and then straddled her. She ran her fingers through Callie's hair as she leaned down and pressed her lips to Callie's.

Everything else ceased to exist when Callie's hands went to her hips and then found their way under her shirt. Taylor moved her hips against her, slowly at first, but when Callie's hands slid up her sides and her thumbs moved across her nipples through her bra, Taylor surged against her. Callie's tongue demanded entry into her mouth, and she parted her lips to take it in. She tried not to let visions of Andrea enter her mind, and was surprised it wasn't more difficult than she thought it would be.

She felt a rush of excitement when Callie reached behind her and unclasped her bra, freeing her breasts for her to take them in her hands. She broke the kiss when Callie gently pinched both of her nipples, her breath ragged.

"Is this okay?" Callie was breathing heavily too. Taylor nodded her response, but she wasn't really sure it was okay. There was something holding her back, and when Callie found the hem of her shirt and tried to lift it over her head, Taylor didn't raise her arms to assist. Callie pulled her head back and looked at her. "What's wrong?"

That was the million-dollar question, wasn't it? Taylor felt panic rising, wondering what the hell she was doing. She'd always thought the memory of Andrea would be what stopped her from being intimate with anyone, but it wasn't in this case. As much as she wanted Callie, she couldn't get past the thought that popped into her head when she tried to remove her shirt.

She's a cop.

Taylor wouldn't—*couldn't*—give her heart away to someone who might leave for work and never make it back home. That kind of pain a second time just might kill her. She shook her head and got to her feet.

"Taylor, what's wrong?" Callie was worried, it was written all over her face. She got to her feet and moved toward Taylor, but Taylor backed away a few steps. "Please talk to me."

"You should go," she said, trying not to cry. "I'm so sorry."

Callie just stood there staring at her, obviously trying to figure out what she'd done wrong. After a few seconds, she finally walked past her and went to the door. Taylor wanted to tell her it wasn't anything she'd done, but the words wouldn't come. The pain she saw in Callie's eyes when she looked back at her almost caused her knees to give out. Without saying a word, Callie walked out the door.

"Jesus, what's wrong with me?" she asked, and Blaze whined from where he was sitting against the couch. Obviously, he was wondering the same thing. She grabbed her phone and called Grace before she could even think about what she was doing.

Chapter Twenty-two

Half an hour after Callie left without even being offered an explanation as to why she'd been tossed out, Taylor opened her front door to let Grace inside. She didn't know Grace nearly as well as she knew Quinn, but they'd spoken many times, and Taylor knew Callie had confided in Grace about what was happening between them. So if Callie trusted Grace, Taylor figured she could too. Besides, she had no desire to have this particular conversation with Quinn after Quinn's little outburst that morning.

"I'm so sorry to have asked you over here like this," Taylor said. She got two cups of coffee and they sat across from each other at the kitchen table.

"It's okay," Grace said with a smile. "What did you want to talk about?"

Where to begin? She wanted to tell her how much she wanted Callie, but given they weren't really close, it seemed silly to do so. But Grace was close with Callie, so why not? It was times like this Taylor wished she'd kept in better contact with the people she'd known from before. But after Andrea died, all she'd wanted was for people to leave her alone. And they did. A few of the firefighters from Andrea's squad tried in the beginning to get her to engage, but even they'd given up after a few months of Taylor's begging them to just let her be.

"I did something really stupid," she said, staring into her coffee cup.

"What did you do?" Grace moved to the chair closer to Taylor and placed a hand on her shoulder. "Does this involve Callie?"

"Yes. We're getting closer, or I guess I should say we *were* getting closer." Taylor sat back and looked at her. "I'm pretty sure I blew any chance I may have had with her."

"I doubt that." Grace smiled at her, and strangely, it made her feel better. "Callie isn't so easily put off. What happened?"

Taylor told her everything, and with every word she spoke, she felt like a weight was being lifted from her shoulders. When she was done, she sat and waited for the words of wisdom she was hoping to get from Grace.

"Okay, wow," she said after what seemed like hours, but in reality had been only a couple of minutes. "She probably assumes you made her leave because of Andrea."

"I know. I should have told her it wasn't about her, but I was afraid of saying something to make the situation worse."

"Well, you told her your hesitation about getting involved with someone in a high-risk profession, so I'm sure she'll understand when you explain it," Grace said, but this wasn't what she'd wanted to hear.

Taylor wasn't even sure what exactly she'd been looking for when she called Grace. She supposed when it came right down to it, she'd simply wanted someone to listen, to tell her everything was going to be fine. But no one could possibly know that. She took a sip of her coffee to try to hide her emotions.

"There is a part of me that does think I'm betraying Andrea," she said quietly.

"I think it's probably a normal feeling, given there hasn't been anyone since her." Grace took her hand and held it. "But sometimes the heart wants something the brain doesn't think it should have. Logically, you know you aren't betraying her, but in your heart it feels like you are. Have you stopped to think perhaps Callie feels the same way? You were her best friend's wife. She might feel as though she's betraying Andrea too."

Taylor looked at her in amazement. This was something she hadn't considered before, but it made perfect sense. She felt an optimism that quickly vanished when she remembered her real reason for telling Callie to leave.

"I don't think I can get past her job."

"You can if you truly have feelings for her." Grace looked at her, obviously waiting for her to say something, but she couldn't. "Do you love her?"

Taylor balked at the question. Love? She knew she cared very much for Callie, and if she were honest, she'd felt this way for quite some time, especially in the months since she'd come back from Atlanta. But love? "I lost the love of my life, Grace. I always assumed we'd grow old together. It was that once in a lifetime kind of love, and I'm not sure I'm capable of loving anyone again."

"Of course you are, sweetie," Grace said with a small smile. "Who says it can't happen *twice* in a lifetime? I can't even imagine losing Quinn, but if something did happen to her, I know she wouldn't want me to spend the rest of my life alone. And honestly, I don't think I could. If I found anyone who made me feel that way again, I'd like to believe I'd be willing to give it a chance. And I really don't think the person's job would even be a consideration. Well, unless she was a criminal, I guess."

Grace laughed, and Taylor couldn't help but laugh along with her. She had an infectious laugh. Just like Quinn.

And just like Callie.

"Does Quinn have any idea how lucky she is to have you?"

"Oh, trust me, I make it a point to remind her every day." Grace winked and sipped her coffee. "Just talk to Callie, okay?

She's an amazing woman. And I'll guarantee she'll understand your hesitation. All you have to do is give her a chance."

Taylor was surprised she actually did feel better after talking to Grace. As soon as she'd left, she tried to call Callie, but she was kicked right to voice mail. She left a message, simply asking her to call her back.

By the time she left to go to the bar, she still hadn't heard from her. She couldn't really blame her though. She'd offered no explanation when she told her to go. Callie was hurt, and it was her fault, which caused a strange ache in her chest. Once she got to the bar, and into her office, she decided to try a text.

Please call me. Let me explain.

After waiting a few minutes, and getting no response, she shoved the phone into her pocket and headed out to the bar to relieve Quinn.

"Hey, boss," Quinn said from where she was leaning against the bar near the cash register.

"You can go on home," Taylor told her as she counted the money in the register. It was dead. There probably wasn't even any reason to stay open. It was Christmas break at the college, and there were less people in the bar now than there had been Thanksgiving weekend. "I'm pretty sure I can handle it on my own."

"No can do." Quinn was shaking her head when Taylor looked at her, and she was smiling. "I talked with Camille, and we decided, at least for a while, you aren't going to be here alone. Your stalker was here earlier asking about you."

"Stalker? I'd hardly call her a stalker," Taylor said, feeling pretty damn good that her employees—her friends—cared about her so much. But she was also irritated they'd decided this without her knowledge. "And I really don't think I need a babysitter."

"Not a babysitter. Think of it more like a bodyguard. I always wanted to be a bodyguard."

"Really?" Taylor quirked an eyebrow at her and knew she sounded skeptical at Quinn's admission.

"I always dreamed about being a Secret Service agent." Quinn smiled, and after a moment she shrugged. "I never did anything to try and make it happen, but I always dreamed about it."

"Go home," Taylor said. "I'm sure Grace is waiting for you."

"I talked to her about all of this, and she agrees with us."

"And you didn't think to consult me on your little plan?"

Taylor felt a modicum of satisfaction when she saw Quinn's cheeks redden slightly.

"I'm sorry," Quinn said, looking down at her feet. "If it makes you feel any better, Callie thinks it's a good idea too."

"When did you talk to Callie about it?" Taylor hoped she didn't sound too interested. There was no need for Quinn to know her feelings. Especially if Callie wasn't going to return her calls. Of course, she knew Grace would probably tell her about their talk anyway.

"About an hour ago. And listen, I'm sorry about this morning. Your private life is none of my business. If you and Callie are seeing each other, then great. I want you both to be happy, okay?"

Taylor nodded, but really only heard some of what Quinn said. She tuned out after hearing she'd talked to Callie an hour ago. When Callie hadn't returned her call, she'd tried convincing herself the battery in her phone had died, or maybe she'd left the phone in her car when she got home. Obviously, that hadn't been the case. Apparently, it was only her Callie didn't want to speak to.

"We don't both need to be here," she said.

"I'm not asking you to pay me for the time. I'll sit at the bar and drink water all night. I just don't think you need to be here alone as long as this woman is going to be hanging around. I have a bad feeling about her."

"Fine," Taylor waved a hand at her and turned to walk back to her office. She pulled her phone out before sitting at her desk, but she knew Callie hadn't called. She decided to try one more time to call, and if she didn't answer or return the call, she wouldn't bother her again.

Just as she was about to place the call, the phone vibrated in her hand. She looked at the display. *Callie.* She took a deep breath and tried to settle her nerves before swiping the screen to accept the call.

"Hi, Callie," she said.

"Hey." Callie didn't sound thrilled to be talking to her, but Taylor chose to ignore it for the time being. She knew Callie had every reason to be put off. "I got your message. You wanted to talk?"

"I wanted to explain what happened."

"You don't need to explain." She still sounded irritated, but her voice had softened a bit. Taylor took it as a good sign. "It's because of Andrea."

"No, Callie, it didn't have anything to do with her, which surprises me, to be perfectly honest."

"Then what?"

Taylor hesitated, but realized there was no reason not to tell her the truth. Complete honesty was something she'd demanded from Andrea, and she wouldn't give Callie any less.

"Your job."

"That isn't going to change, Taylor," she said with a sigh. "It's a part of who I am. Actually, it's a pretty big part of who I am."

"I know, and I'm trying to get past it," Taylor said. The office door opened, and she looked up to see Quinn entering. She held up a hand as she spoke into the phone. "Can you just try and be patient with me? Please?"

"I'll try," Callie said.

"Thank you." Taylor felt lighter than she had when Callie left her house earlier in the afternoon. They ended the call, and she looked at Quinn. "What is it?"

"Sharon's here again." Quinn was on edge, Taylor could tell because of the way the muscles in her jaw clenched. She indicated the phone Taylor still held in her hand. "Was that Callie?"

"Yes, Quinn, it was." She really didn't want to get into this with Quinn. "But it really isn't any of your business."

"I know," Quinn said, seeming to relax as she offered a small smile. "I just thought maybe you should call her back and let her know about your stalker."

"She's not a stalker."

"Not yet."

"Get back to work." Taylor waved her away but remained in her chair for a few moments after she'd gone. There was no way she was going to let this woman intimidate her. It would be nice if she'd get the hint though, and maybe move on. Was that too much to ask?

CHAPTER TWENTY-THREE

"How's Callie doing?" Taylor's mother asked as they sat in the living room Christmas Eve watching the annual showing of *It's a Wonderful Life*. They watched it every year, and Taylor was sure she could probably recite the film word for word.

"She's fine," Taylor said. She was thankful this was the first time since she'd arrived at her parents' house either of them had mentioned Callie.

"Why didn't you bring her with you?" her father asked.

"Seriously, Dad?" Taylor sighed. "I told you we aren't seeing each other. What do I have to do to convince you?"

"It would probably help if you didn't seem so preoccupied since you arrived yesterday," her mother said. "Has something happened between the two of you?"

Taylor simply stared at her mother with her mouth hanging open. How the hell did she do that? She almost wished she'd had kids just so she could figure out how this mother's intuition thing worked. It was scary sometimes.

"Dear," her mother said to her father. "Why don't you go make some popcorn or something?"

"Just tell me to get lost for a few minutes." He chuckled as he got to his feet. "Because I know that's what you're really saying."

He placed a hand on Taylor's shoulder and gave it a gentle squeeze as he walked past her on his way to the kitchen. When he was gone, Taylor turned her attention to her mother.

"Nothing happened between us," she lied. Her mother simply smiled and tilted her head to one side, a sure sign she wasn't buying what Taylor was trying to sell her.

"You can't lie to me, Taylor," she said, amusement in her tone of voice. "Talk to me."

"We kissed a couple of times," Taylor admitted, much to her horror. She couldn't seem to keep any secrets from her mother.

"Are you dating?"

"No."

"Sleeping together?"

"Jesus, Mom," she said, looking away from her when she felt her cheeks flush. "No, we aren't sleeping together."

"Why not?"

Could this get any more embarrassing? She'd never been comfortable talking to her parents about sex, but that never stopped them from asking far too personal questions about her sex life. Her phone started vibrating, and she picked it up to see Callie's name displayed. Perfect timing. Maybe her mother would forget what they were talking about by the time she was done on the phone. Cheeks burning, she stood and went to the guest bedroom so she could talk to her in private.

"Hello," she said.

"Merry Christmas," Callie said.

"Christmas isn't until tomorrow." Taylor smiled. It was good to hear her voice, and she didn't want to think about the reasons why.

"Merry Christmas Eve then," Callie said, and she chuckled. There was a pause, and Callie sighed. "I miss you."

"You're crazy," Taylor said. "You just saw me the night before last."

"I miss seeing you outside the bar."

"Oh." What could she possibly say in response to that? She closed her eyes and tried unsuccessfully to slow her racing heart, but the sound of Callie's voice always did funny things to her insides. Pleasant things.

"I'm sorry, I shouldn't have called."

"It's fine, Callie. I'm happy you called," Taylor said, not wanting to hang up yet. "I miss you, too."

"Really?" Callie asked, sounding a little more upbeat. "Crap…hold on a second."

Taylor waited as Callie talked to someone in the background. How was it possible for just Callie's voice to send a jolt of electricity through her? What the hell was going on with her?

"Sorry about that," Callie said, sounding as though she were smiling. "Meg's kids want me to play Santa Claus."

"Tonight?" Taylor asked. "Wait, aren't they all grown?"

"Yeah, but until earlier this year, they didn't even know Quinn and I existed," Callie said. "And the Santa thing is a family tradition. Everyone gets one present on Christmas Eve. Everything else waits until morning."

"That sounds nice."

"I should probably go," Callie said, sounding reluctant. "Tell your parents I said Merry Christmas."

"You do the same with your family."

"Good-bye, Taylor." Callie didn't wait for her to say good-bye, and the phone went dead in her hand.

It broke her heart to know Callie's sister, Meg, had kept her kids away from their two aunts, simply because they were lesbians. At least they were all getting to know each other now. Taylor found herself wondering if she'd had siblings, would they have been okay with her being gay, or would they have shunned her like Meg and their oldest sister, Beth, had? Maybe she was lucky she was an only child.

She sat on her bed for a moment, wishing she were back in Brockport, celebrating Christmas with Callie. But that was silly, wasn't it? She always spent holidays with her parents. She shook her head and made her way back to the living room.

"Sorry," she said as she resumed her seat on the couch, hoping against hope their earlier conversation had been shelved for the time being.

"Was it Callie?" her mother asked.

"Yes, she said to tell you merry Christmas." Taylor smiled.

"Should I leave the room again?" her father asked.

"Yes," said her mother.

He sighed and went back to the kitchen, and her mother got up to move closer to her on the couch. She took Taylor's hand and held it as she spoke.

"You like her," she said. A statement, not a question. "At Thanksgiving, you said you weren't sure you did."

Taylor started to respond she still wasn't sure of it, but she knew it would be a lie. She didn't know when, or how, it had happened, but yes, she did like Callie. She finally nodded and met her mother's eyes.

"Oh, honey, I know you must be conflicted about this," her mother said as she gathered her into a hug. "You haven't allowed yourself to care about anyone in such a long time. I'm sure Andrea would approve of you falling in love with her best friend."

"Falling in love?" Taylor said, pulling away from her. "Are you crazy? Who said anything about love? I just now admitted I might like her."

"It's obvious you care a great deal about her. And I know you're probably scared, but, honey, you need to allow yourself to feel again."

"I do feel." She looked at her hands and wondered again what was happening to her. "Callie makes me feel."

"Then just let it happen," her mother said. "I know you have reservations about her job, but is it a good reason to deny yourself happiness?"

"I wouldn't survive another loss like that," Taylor said, finally putting into words her deepest fear. At least to her parents. She'd talked around the subject for years, but never came right out with it.

"If you think I didn't worry about your father every time he left the house for work, then you're the one who's crazy," her mother said, smiling affectionately. "But I love him, and his job was a big part of who he was, and who he is now. He wouldn't be the same person without it. And if Callie wasn't with the police department, she probably wouldn't be the same person either. Sometimes you just have to take a chance."

"I don't think I can," Taylor said, her throat tight. Fear was a powerful motivator, and she didn't think she'd be able to do it day in and day out again.

"You're stronger than you think, Taylor," she said, hugging her again. "Don't lose out on something that could be spectacular simply because something *might* happen to her. She could walk out the door right now and get hit by a bus. Nobody knows what the future holds, but if you don't take a chance, you aren't really living."

Callie jumped when she felt a hand on her back, and she turned to see Meg smiling at her. Quinn and Grace had just left, Meg's husband and kids had gone back to their hotel, and she was getting ready to head home as well. They'd all be back bright and early for breakfast in the morning.

"I thought you left with your family," Callie said. "Where's Mom?"

"She's watching TV in the living room," Meg answered. She motioned toward the kitchen table and went to sit. "Talk to me for a few minutes."

"What's up?" Callie asked as she joined her.

"I was going to ask you the same thing," Meg said with a smile. "I've noticed you seemed to be preoccupied all evening. Is something wrong?"

Callie sat back in her chair and studied her sister's face. She couldn't get past the fact Meg had gone along with their oldest sister, Beth, for so many years and not even talked with either her or Quinn. It was almost as though she was trying to make up for lost time, but Beth had now shunned all of them, and she didn't even talk to Meg any longer. When Callie didn't respond, Meg smiled.

"Is it a woman?" she asked.

"Yes," Callie responded.

"Who is it?"

"Quinn's boss. I think you might have met this summer at Quinn's house."

"Taylor?" Meg asked. Callie nodded. "Quinn said she let you stay with her for a few days around Thanksgiving. After you'd been shot. If you'd come to Philly with them, that wouldn't have happened."

"And I wouldn't have gotten to know Taylor better," Callie said.

"So, maybe everything really does happen for a reason." Meg shrugged. "Why aren't you with her tonight?"

"She's at her parents' house. They live a couple of hours away."

Callie went on to tell her everything, and it actually felt good to talk to someone who didn't know her as well as Grace did. And someone who listened better than Quinn and didn't judge her based on her past behavior with women. When she was done, Meg reached across the table and took her hand.

"I think you're doing the right thing, giving her some space and time to really think about things," Meg said. "I know it's hard to be patient in situations like this, but I'm sure she's not only feeling as if she's betraying her late wife, but also that the betrayal is with her late wife's best friend. I can only imagine what she might be going through emotionally."

"She insists it has nothing to do with Andrea," Callie said. "She claims it's because of my career in law enforcement."

"If she truly cares about you, your job won't matter in the end."

"How can you be so sure?"

"I can't. I can only tell you how I would feel if I were in her shoes."

Callie wasn't sure of anything. Except that when Taylor kissed her, she felt more alive than she'd ever felt before in a woman's arms. Being with Taylor meant so much more to her than just sex.

"You're in love with her," Meg said after a moment. Callie opened her mouth to offer a halfhearted protest to the statement, but Meg cut her off. "You should tell her."

"What happened to giving her time and space to figure things out?" Callie asked with a grin. There was no point in denying it. She might not be there yet, but she was definitely falling in love with Taylor.

"There are some things a woman just needs to hear, Callie," she said with a quick squeeze of her hand before letting go. "Maybe knowing where you're at will help her figure out where she wants to be."

"I should go," Callie said as she stood. "You've given me something to think about, and I thank you. Do you need a ride to the hotel?"

"No, I'm staying here to help Mom with breakfast," Meg said. She stood too, and pulled Callie into a hug. "Tell her, Callie. If you don't, she might never figure things out."

Callie nodded but said nothing in response because she wasn't sure she would be able to speak around the lump in her throat. She went and kissed her mother on the cheek then grabbed her coat and headed out to her car.

Maybe Meg was right. Perhaps Taylor needed to hear exactly how Callie was feeling about her. It could send her running in the opposite direction, or it could help to facilitate a turning point in both of their lives.

I do love her, she thought, and she was surprised to realize she'd never felt like this about Jan. She'd obviously settled in that particular relationship, and assumed the love would come later. This time, with Taylor, she knew it could only be a good thing the love had come first.

Chapter Twenty-four

A t some point on her drive back from her parents' house on Christmas night, Taylor made the decision to stop and see Callie. Her mother had succeeded in talking her through her reservations about Callie's job because as she'd pointed out, *you obviously care a great deal about her.*

Yes, it was obvious. It had become even more obvious over the past few days when Callie started coming into the bar every night when her shift ended. Taylor had gotten to the point where she was actually looking forward to the moment she'd walk into the bar because the first sight of Callie each night sent a jolt of arousal through her that made her feel alive. The thought of not seeing her at all on Christmas Eve or on Christmas Day didn't sit well with her.

Which was why she now found herself outside of Grace's bookstore, waiting for Callie to answer the intercom. It was cold out, and Taylor pulled her coat tightly around herself, trying her best to ward off the wind that had steadily picked up over the past couple of hours.

"Yeah?" Callie's voice came through the intercom, and Taylor smiled at the warmth she felt just hearing it.

"It's Taylor," she said as she pushed the button. "Let me in before I freeze to death."

Callie didn't respond, and there was enough of a period of silence for Taylor to second-guess her decision to drop by unannounced. What if Callie wasn't alone? She shook her head. Callie had promised to try to be patient while she worked through the issues she was having with her job. She'd seen nothing from Callie since the promise had been made to make her think there was anyone else on her radar. Even knowing that, she held her breath in the few moments she spent waiting for Callie to buzz her in.

The sound of a door closing above the bookstore caused her to wonder again if Callie might have company. She heard footsteps hurrying down the staircase right inside the door, and then there was Callie, wearing shorts and a T-shirt. And a big smile that let Taylor know she was happy to see her.

"I'm sorry it took so long, but the button to unlock this door isn't working," she said as she took Taylor by the elbow and pulled her inside. "Damn, it's cold out there."

"Maybe you should have some clothes on," Taylor said, allowing her gaze to sweep her body slowly before settling on Callie's smiling eyes.

"And miss having you look at me like that?" Callie shook her head and turned to go back up the stairs. Taylor struggled to not stare at her ass as she followed. "Not a chance."

"I was only here once, but I was a little pissed off and didn't really take the time to let it all sink in," Taylor said upon entering the apartment and looking around. "This is…cozy."

"Very diplomatic way of putting it," Callie said with a chuckle. "Welcome to my bedroom."

"That is pretty much what it is, isn't it?" Taylor's line of sight moved no farther than the bed against the wall. There was absolutely nowhere else to sit.

"I sleep here, and I shower here. It has everything I need." Callie went and moved her laptop off the bed and straightened the sheets and blanket before offering her a seat. "Sorry I can't offer something more comfortable."

"This is fine." Taylor removed her coat and hung it on a hook by the door. A few steps in and she was at the foot of the bed. She looked at Callie, who was still smiling.

"Do you want something to drink?" she asked, heading toward what Taylor assumed was the kitchen. There was a refrigerator in one corner, a stove next to it, and a microwave on what little counter space there was. A very small sink appeared as though it might have actually been an afterthought.

"Water?" Taylor asked.

"Are you sure? I have beer, or wine if you want."

"Water is good," she said, taking a seat on the edge of the bed. She didn't want alcohol to take the blame for what she was planning. She took a deep breath and watched Callie coming back to the bed with two bottles of water in her hand. She handed one to Taylor and took a seat, leaving about a foot between them. "Merry Christmas."

"Merry Christmas," Callie replied. They touched their bottles together in a toast. "So, to what do I owe the pleasure of your company on this God-awful frigid night?"

"I wanted to see you," Taylor said, a little surprised at her admission.

"Nice," Callie said with a nod. "I'm glad you did."

"I'm not interrupting anything?"

Callie almost spit her water out as she laughed and looked around the room.

"Really? Does it look like you are?"

"You took a while to open the door."

"You think I'm not wearing enough clothing now, you should have seen me before you got here. I was lounging around in my underwear. I grabbed the first thing I found to put on so I could go downstairs and let you in."

"I see," Taylor said, looking at the expanse of toned thigh within touching distance. She swallowed and looked away when Callie stared at her, an unreadable expression on her face.

Callie tilted her head to the side and studied her intently. Taylor fought to not meet her gaze because she thought it might very well be her undoing. Callie took her hand and raised it to her lips, placing a kiss on her knuckles.

"You thought I might have had someone else here," she said quietly.

Taylor almost said no, but when she turned her head, the look in Callie's eyes told her everything she needed to know. Her breath hitched at the look of desire she was sure mirrored her own.

"Just for a moment, I wondered," Taylor admitted, feeling her face heat with embarrassment.

Callie moved closer to her and pulled her into her arms. "You never have to wonder, baby," she said into Taylor's ear, the warm breath causing goose bumps to form on her arms. "I said I'd be patient with you while you tried to work this out, and I meant it. I don't want anyone else."

"Good to know," Taylor said, pulling back enough to kiss her. The moan Callie made when her tongue entered her mouth caused a rush of wetness between Taylor's legs. She leaned into Callie until she was on her back, and Taylor was on top of her. "It's also a good thing this bed is your only furniture."

"I never knew it would come in so handy," Callie smiled briefly before taking her lips again. Her legs spread beneath her, and Taylor jolted at the feel of their pelvic bones pressing together.

"God, you feel so good," Taylor said. She'd never felt so alive.

"I think I could kiss you forever," Callie said as she put a hand behind Taylor's head and captured her lips once again.

Taylor groaned into her mouth when Callie's legs wrapped around her, holding her where she was. She tried to get a hand between them, almost desperate to feel Callie, but there was no room for it. She broke the kiss and looked at her until Callie opened her eyes.

"I need to touch you," she said, her breath ragged, and her voice sounding almost desperate to her own ears. "I need you to touch me."

"Are you sure this time?" Callie looked uncertain, and Taylor knew she was responsible for the tentative question.

She got to her feet and began removing her clothes while Callie watched her from the bed, her elbows supporting her and a lazy grin tugging at her lips. But it was her eyes, and the pure desire she saw there, that emboldened Taylor.

"I promise you I've never been this sure of anything in my life," Taylor said. She expected to feel a twinge of guilt at the admission she hadn't been this sure even about Andrea. But it didn't come. She pushed the thought from her mind and dropped her shirt on the floor. She kicked off her shoes and slid her pants down to step out of them. "Are *you* sure?"

"God, yes," Callie said. She sat up and reached for Taylor, pulling her closer and pressing her lips to her abdomen. "You're so fucking amazing."

Taylor ran her fingers through Callie's hair, holding her head where it was. She tensed when Callie's hands moved up her back and unhooked her bra. She wasn't sure how much longer she'd be able to stand. Her legs began to tremble as Callie slid the straps down her arms, and the bra joined the rest of her clothes on the floor. She took a step back and removed her underwear. She felt Callie's eyes on her as though it were a physical touch, and Taylor fought to keep from crossing her arms over her chest.

Her nipples hardened when Callie got to her feet and took a step toward her, but she held a hand out to stop her as she shook her head.

"I need to touch you," Callie said, her eyes pleading, but Taylor simply pointed at her.

"You have far too many clothes on to be a part of this," she said, expecting her to make short work of shedding her shorts and T-shirt. Instead, Callie sat back down.

"Then I'll just watch you touch yourself while you wonder what it would feel like for me to be doing it," she said with a smirk.

"Not an option, smartass," Taylor said. She picked up her bra and started to put it back on, hoping Callie wouldn't call her bluff because she really didn't want to leave like this. "I can just go home."

Callie stood and peeled off her shirt before pushing her shorts down and stepping out of them. She wasn't wearing a bra, and Taylor actually felt her mouth water at the sight of her standing there completely naked. She let her own bra fall to the floor once again when their eyes met. She looked down at the scar on Callie's shoulder. The scar she would forever associate with the moment she'd started falling for her. She reached out and touched it gently.

"Does it still hurt?" she asked, meeting Callie's eyes.

"No," Callie said softly. "Not really."

Taylor watched as Callie walked around to the other side of the bed and got under the covers. She propped herself up on an elbow, her head resting in her hand. With her other hand, she pulled back the covers and patted the bed.

"You should join me," she said. "It's much warmer in here than it is out there."

Taylor got in and stretched out alongside her, fully intending to push her onto her back, but Callie was too quick for her. Before she knew what was happening Callie was on top of her, straddling her hips, and Taylor had to admit she liked it. She ran her hands up Callie's torso and pinched her nipples lightly.

"Oh, yeah," Callie breathed, her center sliding along Taylor's lower abdomen.

Taylor groaned at the feel of the slick heat covering her, and she was happy to realize she'd caused this in such an incredible and beautiful woman.

"You're so wet, and so freaking beautiful," she murmured, still pinching Callie's nipples because it was obvious the harder she did it, the more Callie thrust against her. Callie's hands came down on the bed on either side of her head, and she rested their foreheads together.

"It's all you, baby," she said before closing her eyes and swallowing. "It is *all* you."

Callie eased away from her, and Taylor just managed to stop herself from whimpering at the loss of contact. She did whimper when Callie pushed a knee between her legs and spread them before kissing each nipple and then moving slowly down her torso.

Taylor gripped the sheets and tilted her head back when she felt Callie's breath on her center, and thought she might shatter into a million pieces when Callie's tongue found her clit then sucked it between her lips.

"Fuck, Callie," she said, panting. Callie put a forearm over her abdomen to hold her down, and then slowly slid a finger inside her. After a moment of the tantalizing torture she inflicted on her clit, alternately sucking and biting, Callie added a second finger. Taylor cried out when she slowly pulled her fingers almost all the way out before thrusting them in again. She spread her legs farther, still gripping the sheets tightly, and they began a slow rhythm that only got faster and more urgent the closer Taylor came to soaring over the edge.

"Yes, oh, God, Callie," she said, one hand moving to the back of Callie's head to make sure she stayed in that exact spot. It felt so damn good. Callie gave one last thrust, sucked hard on her clit, and then Taylor felt such an indescribable rush of overwhelming heat and ecstasy that started in her center and spread out through her limbs. When she finally came down, she realized she was still holding Callie's head and laughed as she let go of her. Callie looked at her and smiled. "I'm so sorry."

"Don't ever be sorry." Callie placed a quick kiss on her clit and climbed up to lay next to her. "Trust me when I say I could stay there forever. You have absolutely nothing to apologize for."

"I could have smothered you."

"Yeah," Callie said before running her tongue up her neck to her ear. She tugged on her earlobe with her teeth. "But what a way to go."

"Stop," Taylor said, reaching down to grab Callie's hand which was moving dangerously close to her sex again. Callie chuckled in her ear and she brought the hand up to rest on her breast. "I need some recovery time, tiger."

"Okay, okay," Callie said. "Maybe we should nap."

"Are you serious?" Taylor gave her a look she knew portrayed her disbelief at the remark.

"What?" Callie looked innocent as she pulled back and looked at her, but Taylor knew better.

She pushed her onto her back and kissed her. Not a gentle kiss, but one she hoped carried the depth of what she was feeling. Callie moaned into her mouth.

"Still want to nap?" Taylor asked with a grin.

"Fuck, no," Callie answered, letting her legs open wide to allow Taylor's hand the access she desired.

CHAPTER TWENTY-FIVE

Callie groaned when she opened her eyes and was met with the bright sunshine coming through the window. She closed them again and snuggled into the naked body pressed against her back. Memories of the night before flooded her senses, and she groaned again, but this time in happiness.

"Good morning."

The body moved away from her, and Callie rolled over onto her back, looking up at the most beautiful woman she'd ever had the good fortune to lay eyes on. She reached up and caressed her cheek. When Taylor had shown up the night before, Callie had been so surprised. She'd gotten to the point where she looked forward to going to the bar every night just to see her. It had taken her all day to convince herself she wouldn't be seeing her, and then there she was. And then there she was, *naked.*

Callie closed her eyes at the onslaught of arousal at the memory, and then had to laugh at herself. Taylor touched her face, causing her to open her eyes again.

"What?" she asked, a small smile touching her lips.

"Nothing," Callie said and tried to get up, but Taylor had other ideas. She threw a leg over her so she couldn't move.

"You aren't going anywhere until you tell me why you were laughing."

"I was just wondering how I could possibly be turned on again after spending the vast majority of the past..." she paused and lifted her head to look at the clock by the bed, "...wow, fourteen hours? Can that possibly be right?"

"Yep." Taylor smiled. "You were saying?"

"We've spent the past fourteen hours getting to know each other a whole lot better, and yet I want you again. And no doubt again after that." Callie pulled her over on top of her and kissed her. "How can that be possible?"

"I don't know," Taylor said with a shrug. "I guess twenty-seven orgasms aren't enough to keep you sated."

"Twenty-seven, huh?" Callie smirked. "You think quite a lot of yourself, don't you?"

"Shouldn't I?"

"Most definitely, but I highly doubt it was that many. Just on the off chance though, maybe we should try for twenty-eight." She smiled when Taylor nodded enthusiastically. "Or fifty?"

"Don't push your luck, tiger."

"Don't you need to get home and let Blaze out?"

"Trying to get rid of me so soon?"

"No, I'd be perfectly happy to have you right here in my bed for at least the rest of the year." Callie nipped her chin playfully. "I just don't want Blaze to start hating me."

"I don't think you have to worry about that happening," Taylor said. "But I left him with my parents for a few days. They're coming here on New Year's Eve, so they'll bring him back then. But I think it's awfully sweet of you to worry about him."

Callie's phone started ringing then, and Taylor tensed. Callie knew she assumed it was work, so she decided to ignore it because it was obvious Taylor hadn't worked out *all* the reservations about Callie's job. If it was important, whoever it was would leave a message or call back. Callie was intent on showing Taylor she was more important than the job.

"You need to answer it?" Taylor asked as Callie put her arms around her and held her closer. She placed a few kisses on Taylor's neck and moaned.

"No, all I need is you," she said.

Taylor relaxed against her and Callie sighed in contentment as Taylor reached a hand between them and cupped her sex. When her fingers slipped inside, Callie forgot about everything but how incredibly good it felt to have Taylor's naked body on top of her own.

The next night, after Callie finished her shift, she went right to the bar. She knew Quinn and Camille weren't going to leave Taylor alone, but after the two nights they'd spent together, she felt an overpowering need to protect her. And she'd seriously hated the fact she had to leave her that morning in order to go into work. When she walked in, Quinn waved at her, and she went to sit at the bar.

"How's it going?" Quinn asked as she set a beer in front of her.

"Not bad," Callie grinned. They hadn't seen or spoken to each other since dinner on Christmas Day. "Not bad at all."

Quinn gave her an odd look, but didn't say anything. She went to get a drink for another customer but kept looking over at Callie, no doubt trying to figure out why she was grinning like a fool. Callie knew the exact moment she'd figured it out. She watched in amusement as Quinn was forced to finish with her customer before she could come back to her.

"Holy shit," Quinn said as she leaned on the bar and tried not to smile. "I've been wondering all night why Taylor seems different, and then you show up all smiles."

"And?" Callie asked before taking a sip of her beer.

"You're really going to make me say it?"

"You didn't have a problem asking me before," she said, referring to the day she'd brought Taylor to brunch at their mother's.

"You aren't going to let me live that down, are you?" Quinn grimaced, and Callie shook her head. "I said I was sorry."

"It was rude and it was crude, Quinn. Although I really should just expect it from you by now."

"You slept with her," Quinn said. "Am I right?"

"Yes, but don't say anything to her about it," Callie answered. "I think she still has a problem with my job. And besides, I'm sure if she wants you to know, she'll tell you."

Quinn nodded, then her head turned to the front door and she frowned. Callie followed her gaze and tensed when she saw Sharon walk in.

"She's been here every night for the past two weeks," Callie said when she looked back at Quinn. "Does she ever say anything to you?"

"She always asks about Taylor." Quinn shook her head. "I tell her Taylor isn't her concern, and then she just stares at me the rest of the night, but doesn't say anything else."

"Send her a drink on me," Callie said. Quinn looked at her like she'd lost her mind, but she made the drink and delivered it to her. Callie watched as Quinn glanced over her shoulder and pointed to her. Sharon just nodded once to acknowledge her.

"Please tell me you didn't just buy her a drink," Taylor said into her ear as Callie felt her arms come around her waist. She reached down and covered Taylor's hands with her own against her abdomen.

"I wanted to make sure she knew I was here," Callie said, turning her head to the side so she could see her.

"I wish she'd just stop coming here," Taylor said. To Callie's surprise, Taylor gave her a quick kiss on the lips before letting go of her and sitting on the stool next to her. "It's really getting kind of creepy."

"Has she said something to you? She hasn't threatened you, has she?" Callie asked, unable to hide the concern she felt.

"No, she just stares at me whenever I come out here. Like I said, creepy."

Callie watched Taylor as her gaze dropped to her lips, and her pulse rate jumped noticeably. She smiled and shook her head.

"All you have to do is look at me and I get turned on," Callie said.

"Good to know," Taylor said with a wink. She put a hand on Callie's thigh and moved it higher before dipping between her legs. Callie closed her eyes at the onslaught of desire and tightened her legs to keep her hand there. "Come home with me tonight."

"God, yes," Callie said. "I'd do anything for you."

"Also good to know." Taylor laughed.

"Am I going to have to hose you two down?" Quinn asked with a good-natured smile.

"Maybe," Taylor said as she pulled her hand away from Callie's body. It surprised Callie to know Taylor wasn't trying to deny what was happening between them.

"I need to change a keg," Quinn said with a chuckle. "I assume you two will be able to keep your hands off each other for a few minutes?"

"I promise nothing of the kind, but go," Taylor said. When Quinn was gone, Taylor kissed Callie on the cheek and stood up. "I have to get something from the office. I'll be back in a minute."

Callie watched her walking away, appreciating the view. When she looked back to her beer, she saw Sharon walking to the bathroom, which was down the same hallway as the office. Without thinking, she got up and followed her.

She watched as Sharon stopped outside the restroom door, but then looked toward the office. She turned and walked the few steps to the door before reaching out and grabbing the doorknob.

"Can I help you?" Callie asked, about ten feet behind her. Sharon jumped and turned to face her, and she was obviously not happy.

"I was looking for the restroom," she said, pretending to be embarrassed. She looked pointedly at the sign which said *Office,* then at the door that said *Ladies,* which she then went to. "Guess I overshot it a bit."

Callie said nothing as she watched her go into the bathroom, but she stood there waiting until Taylor came out of the office.

"What are you doing?" Taylor asked as she approached her. Instead of answering, Callie took her by the hand and led her back to the bar.

"She followed you," Callie said. She sat back down on her bar stool, and Taylor went behind the bar to get a customer a draft beer.

"What?"

"She was about to open the door to the office when I asked her if I could help her."

"Where is she now?" Taylor asked when she came back around the bar to sit next to Callie.

"Bathroom. I think from now on, whenever you go to the office, you should lock the door behind you." Callie could tell by the look on her face she wasn't happy with the suggestion, but after a moment, she nodded her agreement.

"I hate this," she said after Sharon walked past them and back to her seat at the far end of the bar.

"I know," Callie said. She put a hand on Taylor's back and smiled when she leaned into the touch. "I hate it too. She's getting a little more brazen though, so hopefully she'll do something to screw up and I can have the Brockport Police haul her ass in."

"I just hope nobody gets hurt in the process." Taylor turned and took Callie's face between her hands and forced her to look at her. "Especially you."

"I was thinking the same thing about you," Callie said. "I don't want to lose you now that I've found you."

"How about we get out of here?" Taylor said with a smile. "I'm sure Quinn won't mind closing."

"Lead the way."

Chapter Twenty-six

Callie woke up in the middle of the night and looked at the clock. Three thirty. She threw the covers off, intending to go to the bathroom, but an arm went around her torso and held her where she was.

"Where do you think you're going?" Taylor asked before kissing her on the shoulder.

"Bathroom?" Callie said with a grin. But she didn't have to go anymore. There were other things going on in her body that were more demanding at the moment. She turned on her side and pulled Taylor closer before kissing her. "It can wait."

"Why is it I can't seem to get enough of you?" Taylor whispered.

"I don't know, but I'm having the same problem," Callie said. "Not that it's truly a problem, mind you."

Taylor moaned when Callie reached between them and slid two fingers through her wetness. When she went inside, Taylor rolled onto her back and her legs fell open, and Callie moved on top of her.

"No," Taylor said with a lazy smile. "Definitely not a problem."

It only took a few moments before Callie felt Taylor tightening around her fingers, and she squeezed her ass, causing Callie's hips to surge forward, and she came along with her.

They dozed again, and it was light out when Callie next opened her eyes. She turned to look at Taylor, but she was alone in the bed. She sat up, and that was when she noticed the smell of coffee in the air. She smiled as she put her clothes on and then headed toward the kitchen.

"Good morning," she said, walking up behind Taylor at the sink and hugging her. Taylor let her head fall back against her shoulder and smiled.

"Good morning," she answered. "You're lucky you woke up when you did. I was actually thinking about making breakfast, and I promise you, it would not have turned out well."

"You have food to make breakfast?" Callie asked, surprised.

"I do," she answered. "When you left for work yesterday, I went to the store before coming home and I bought bacon and eggs. Real food, can you believe it?"

"Wow, I'm impressed." Callie released her and went to look in the refrigerator to find a dozen eggs and a package of bacon. She grabbed them and set them on the counter before turning to her again, a smile on her face. "Pretty confident you were going to get me to come home with you last night, weren't you?"

Taylor shrugged and gave her a smile of her own. "I guess if you'd turned me down I'd have had to learn how to cook. This," she said, pointing at the eggs and bacon, "would have been practice for next time."

"I don't think I would ever turn you down," Callie admitted. "You could probably get me to do pretty much anything."

"Then how about we go back to bed and do breakfast later?"

"I wish I could," Callie said reluctantly. "But I have to go to work."

"Okay," Taylor said, tensing slightly. She turned away and poured them each a cup of coffee. She took them both to the table and sat down. "Are you back on the streets yet, or are you still assigned to desk duty?"

"Still riding the desk for now," Callie said as she joined her. She wished she could make Taylor feel better about her job, but didn't have a clue how to go about it. "You know I'd rather stay here with you all day, right?"

Taylor nodded but wouldn't meet her eyes. Callie sighed, not liking the distance between them at the mention of her work.

"I'm sorry," Taylor said, shaking her head. "I'm still dealing with some reservations about the job, but I'm getting there, okay?"

"Okay," Callie nodded. "I guess I should make breakfast."

They ate quickly and then Callie rushed home to shower and get ready for work. Taylor washed the dishes after she'd gone and then went to make the bed, upset with herself for making things tense between them.

She sat on the edge of the bed and grabbed Callie's pillow, holding it up to her face and inhaling the scent of her. She closed her eyes at the arousal the scent prompted. She put the pillow back and grabbed the picture of her and Andrea she'd laid face down on the nightstand the night before.

"What am I doing, baby?" she asked the smiling face of her late wife. "God, I just hope you understand I need to move on. I fought it for as long as I could, but Callie…" She sighed and wiped the tears from her face. "She's a good person, but you knew that, didn't you? You never would have been friends with her if she wasn't. Please understand."

She lost the fight to stop her tears as she carried the framed picture out to the living room and placed it on the bookshelf where she had other pictures of Andrea, as well as her parents. She shook her head but never took her eyes from the photograph.

"I will always love you," she said quietly.

❖

"Okay, spill, Burke," Harry said when he walked up to her desk later that day.

"What the hell are you talking about?" she asked, looking up from the boring paperwork she was trying to concentrate on.

"You were different yesterday," he said, sitting on the corner of the desk and looking down at her. She leaned back and crossed her arms. "You were smiling. As a matter of fact, you're still smiling. So spill."

"I don't know what you're talking about," she said innocently. Things had been tense between her and Taylor before she'd left for work, but it hadn't stopped her mind from running a continuous loop of the two of them in bed. She couldn't help but smile.

"You got laid," he said.

"Jesus, Chambers. Crude much?"

"Oh, believe me, there are much cruder ways I could have phrased it." He smiled, and Callie knew he finally figured it out. "Taylor Fletcher? The crazy lady who talks to herself?"

"She's not crazy," Callie said defensively.

"She is if she's sleeping with you, Burke," Harry said, laughing. She glared at him, which only succeeded in making him laugh more. "Oh, come on, admit it. You walked right into that one."

"I did," she said, unable to stop from laughing along with him. "But I assure you, there's very little sleeping going on."

He stopped laughing and she watched as his cheeks turned red. Really? Harry Chambers was embarrassed by a vague reference to sex?

"And you, my friend, walked right into that one," she said.

"Burke, Chambers, we've got a murder, and you're up," their lieutenant said as she walked up to the desk. She looked at Callie and smiled. "You ready to get back on the horse?"

"Yes, ma'am," she said as she stood. "Absolutely."

"Don't go getting yourself shot again, you hear me?"

Harry laughed again, and Callie just glared at him. He was still laughing as he went to get his jacket. Amanda put a hand on Callie's arm before she could grab her own jacket.

"I mean it, Burke," she said, a stern look on her face. "You need to be more careful out there. I don't want to lose anyone."

"You won't lose me," Callie assured her. Besides, she knew Taylor would never forgive her if she got shot again. She planned to do everything by the book from now on because she was hoping to make a life with Taylor, if she could ever convince her she was playing it safe at work.

CHAPTER TWENTY-SEVEN

Callie walked into the bar that night full of trepidation over having to tell Taylor she was back on the streets. Not knowing how Taylor was going to react was wreaking all kinds of havoc on her gut. She breathed a sigh of relief at seeing Quinn behind the bar, and there was no sign of Taylor.

"I just want water," she said when Quinn grabbed a glass and headed for the beer taps. Quinn looked at her strangely, and Callie shook her head. "My stomach is a mess."

"What's going on?" Quinn asked.

"I have to tell Taylor I'm back on full duty."

"She had to know this was coming, right?" Quinn asked. She leaned on the bar and glanced quickly toward the office, presumably to make sure Taylor wasn't going to sneak up behind her. "You guys have talked about it, right?"

"Not really." Callie put her elbows on the bar and rested her head in her hands. The churning in her gut made her feel like she was going to be sick. "We've both kind of danced around it, thinking it might just go away, I guess."

"Well, that's mature." Quinn chuckled and poked Callie's forearm to get her to look at her. "You really think it's going to be a problem?"

"I don't know," Callie said with a shrug. She sighed and closed her eyes for a moment. "I think things are good between us, except she gets obviously upset when I say anything about work. It's like she's okay with it as long as it's never talked about."

"What are you two talking about so seriously?" Taylor asked from the end of the bar where neither of them had seen her approach.

Quinn straightened quickly and grabbed a towel to start wiping down the bar after she shot Callie a quick look that said *good luck*. Callie watched her as she walked away, and she had to stifle a groan when she felt Taylor's hand on her shoulder before she gave her a quick kiss on the cheek.

"What's going on?" she asked again.

Callie turned to face her and forced a smile. "Nothing's going on. Why?"

"I'm not stupid, Callie," she said, one eyebrow raised.

"Can we talk in your office?" Callie didn't want to have this discussion, but she knew it would be better to just do it and be done with it. She just hoped Taylor wouldn't shut her out.

"Okay, wow," Taylor said, looking as worried as Callie felt. "This must be serious."

Callie glanced at Quinn as she stood to follow Taylor to the office. Once the door was closed, the air was thick with apprehension, and Callie wasn't sure where to begin. She waited for Taylor to take a seat at her desk before grabbing the only other chair in the room and pulling it over so she could sit next to her.

"You're really starting to worry me, Callie," Taylor said when the silence obviously got to be too much.

Callie leaned forward, her hands clasped in her lap, and took a deep breath. The only way to do it was quickly, like ripping off a Band-Aid, something her mother always liked to say. After a moment, she met Taylor's eyes.

"I'm back on full duty."

Taylor tensed, and Callie felt the air shift around them. Taylor was staring at her, and Callie refused to look away, afraid if she did, Taylor might just vanish. Her breathing quickened as she waited for some kind of response. *Anything* would be preferable to the silence surrounding them and seeming to cut off her oxygen.

"When?"

"Today. This morning. I thought about calling you, but figured it could wait until tonight." Callie felt as though she were rambling. She closed her mouth and waited again.

"I can't do this," Taylor said as she shook her head slowly. Callie felt her heart break a little at her words. That and the tears welling up in Taylor's eyes almost caused the same reaction from her. "I can't."

"Baby, we can make this work."

"No." Taylor stood and walked toward the door. She faced Callie again before opening it and walking out. "You don't understand. This is like an open wound for me, Callie. I thought I'd figured things out, but I guess I haven't. I just can't do this. I can't risk that pain again."

Callie slumped back in the chair when Taylor left without another word. Without giving Callie the opportunity to say anything in her own defense. Who was she kidding? Nothing she could have said would change the way Taylor felt. Maybe it was better to end things now than to do it later, when she'd fallen completely.

"Too late," she whispered, letting the tears fall.

"Are you okay?" Quinn asked, her voice full of concern.

"No," Taylor answered, shaking her head but managing to not cry. Damn it, she'd really thought she could deal with

Callie's job. She'd been shot just over a month earlier, and who could say it wouldn't happen again, but with deadly results? As long as Callie had been on desk duty, she'd been able to convince herself everything would be fine. But now? Not so much, apparently.

"Where's Callie?" Quinn asked her.

"The office." Taylor forced herself to meet Quinn's gaze. "Can you please get her to leave? I don't think I can."

Quinn nodded, and Taylor felt a sense of relief knowing she could count on Quinn. She got drinks for a couple of people at the bar and tried not to look in the direction of the office, but when Callie and Quinn appeared, she found she couldn't look away. The sadness in Callie's eyes was obvious, and Taylor felt her heart clench. She turned her head, but Callie came to the bar and leaned across it.

"I'll go, for now, but as long as Sharon is still hanging around here, I'll be in every night when I get off work. I'll give you your space, but I won't leave you alone so she can hurt you."

And then she was gone. Just like that. And honestly, she wasn't entirely sure it hurt any less than it had when Andrea died.

Chapter Twenty-eight

Taylor looked at the clock behind her and sighed. It was the night before New Year's Eve, and she just wanted to go home. The next night was going to be a bitch, just like it was every year, college kids or not. Quinn had wanted to stay, but Taylor convinced her since Callie was there, she didn't need to hang around.

It had been two days since she ended things with Callie, but true to her word, she was coming in every night, because Sharon was still making nightly visits. They didn't talk any more than was necessary, and there was no touching anymore, which made Taylor inexplicably sad.

There was only one customer in the place, Randy, and he was sitting at the end of the bar. Since it was only a little after midnight, she knew she couldn't ask him to leave. He'd been coming in pretty regularly since the first night she'd seen him, the first night Sharon had made her presence known.

Taylor knew Callie had been wary of him at first, thinking perhaps he'd known Sharon, and they were just working on setting Taylor up for something. But since the night he'd told her he was a cop too, Callie had spent a lot of time talking with him whenever they were there at the same time.

"One more?" he asked with a smile. "Then I'll go so you can close up a little early."

Taylor nodded with a smile and filled a glass. She leaned on the bar to talk to him just as she heard the front door open. *Fantastic. Another customer.* She turned her head and almost groaned when she saw Sharon taking a seat at the bar.

"Fuck me," she murmured under her breath.

"Sorry," Randy said. "I guess I should have just left. Let you close before she got here."

"Not your fault," she assured him before turning and walking over to her. She wished Callie would get back from the bathroom already. "What can I get you?"

"The usual," she answered with a smile. Taylor hated the fact she knew what *the usual* was for this woman. She quickly mixed her drink and took her money. She turned to walk away when Sharon's voice stopped her.

"No girlfriend tonight?" she asked, sounding downright pleased with the notion.

Taylor didn't answer, but simply smiled at her.

"And no bodyguards either?" Sharon winked at her, causing Taylor to cringe inwardly. "Must be my lucky night. I was beginning to think I'd never have a shot with you. Maybe you should ask him to leave. You know, so we can be alone."

Taylor just stared at her, amazed by her brazenness.

"I don't think so," she finally managed to say.

"Oh, I'm sorry. Did that sound like a request?" She moved her jacket just enough so Taylor could see the gun she was carrying. "You can get rid of him, or I can. It's up to you. And don't even think about telling him I have a gun."

Taylor walked to the other end of the bar, honestly surprised she was able to do it on her shaking legs. She forced a smile at Randy and noticed Sharon moved closer, no doubt to make sure she didn't mention the gun.

"I'm sorry, Randy, but I'm going to have to ask you to leave," she managed to say in a steady voice. She unplugged her phone, which had been charging, and handed it to him. "Here's your phone." Now she found herself hoping Callie didn't come back from the bathroom. She wouldn't want them both to be in danger. She forced a smile. "Sharon and I would like to be alone."

The look Randy gave her alleviated her fear that he wouldn't understand what was going on. He glanced at Sharon and smiled at both of them.

"Sure thing," he said as he got to his feet. He walked out of the bar without looking back, which obviously helped to relax Sharon a bit.

"Good job," she said with a nod. "Now you're going to go to the office and get your things, and you and I are going on a little road trip."

"I'm not going anywhere with you," Taylor said, speaking a little louder than necessary. Her hope was Callie might hear them and know to not just walk right out there into the middle of what could easily turn into a volatile situation. Especially with a cop thrown into the mix.

"Feisty, huh?" Sharon laughed as she came behind the bar and pulled her gun out, shoving it into Taylor's ribs. "Usually, I admire that in a woman, but right now, you just need to do as I say, or else you won't be going anywhere again. Ever."

Taylor tried to pull away from her, but Sharon held her arm tightly as she leaned in close to her ear.

"I promise you, you'll soon forget your girlfriend, which shouldn't be too hard, because I've noticed there's been some distance between the two of you lately. I can make you feel things you never thought possible." She laughed before kissing her on the cheek. "But only if you don't make me shoot you. Don't think I won't if you decide not to cooperate."

"Let me go!" Taylor yelled. She tried in vain to push her away, but Sharon merely laughed again before backhanding her across the face with the gun held in her hand. Taylor cried out as she fell to the floor, the pain exploding in her head. She refused to pass out because the thought of what could possibly happen if she did scared her to death.

"You fucking bitch!" Sharon yelled before kicking her hard in the ribs. "Why did you make me hit you?"

Taylor looked up to see her opening the register and taking out all the cash, shoving it into her pockets. She grabbed Taylor's arm and tried to pull her to her feet, but Taylor wasn't about to go along blindly with this obviously unstable woman.

"Get up!" she screamed.

Taylor wasn't sure how much longer she'd be able to stay conscious. She just hoped to God Callie knew what was going on and would come to her rescue. The irony of the situation didn't escape her. All along she'd been worried about Callie's job being dangerous. Now here she was, being held at gunpoint, and she almost laughed at the absurdity of it all. With amazing clarity, she realized she loved Callie. Job or no job, she loved her. She just hoped she lived long enough to be able to tell her.

Callie heard the commotion coming from the bar area when she shut off the water after washing her hands. She took her phone out and called Taylor, but after a couple of rings it went straight to voice mail. Just as she was reaching for the doorknob, her phone vibrated in her hand. She let out a sigh of relief when she saw Taylor's name on the display.

"Taylor, what the hell is going on?" she asked, her hand still on the doorknob.

"Listen to me, Callie, this is Randy," came the voice from the other end of the line.

"Why do you have her phone?"

"Sharon came in. I don't know what her game is, but she made Taylor get me to leave. She slipped her phone to me, I assumed so I could call you." Randy was talking quickly, and Callie was having a hard time keeping up.

All she could think about was that Taylor was in serious trouble. She cursed herself for having left her gun in the trunk of her car.

"I need to help her," Callie said, sounding almost helpless to her own ears. "I have to go out there and help her."

"No, listen," Randy said. "I already called the Brockport Police. They should be here any second. You need to stay put and wait for help to arrive. You won't be able to do anything for her if Sharon gets you too."

Callie knew he was right, but her heart was racing. She remembered Quinn telling her once that Taylor kept a handgun in the office. She had no idea where it was, but she wasn't going to hunker down in the bathroom when she had a chance to help her. She promised Randy she'd stay where she was and then shoved her phone in her pocket, thankful she'd had the sound turned off so Sharon couldn't have heard it ring.

She gripped the doorknob tighter and closed her eyes as she turned it, praying Sharon wouldn't be able to hear her. She pulled the door open and looked down the hall toward the bar. There was no sign of anyone, and it was quiet out there. She hadn't heard any commotion outside the restroom door, so she was pretty confident they hadn't made their way to the office.

She walked quickly and as quietly as she could to the office door and opened it, slipped inside, and shut it as softly as she could, then she flipped on the light switch. She began her search in the desk, but there was no gun in any of the drawers. She glanced around the office wondering where the hell it could be, and stopped when she saw Andrea's firefighter helmet sitting on a shelf.

She moved to the shelves and picked it up. She smiled. It was there, right underneath the helmet. Was it possible Andrea was looking out for them? She put her hand over her heart and looked at the ceiling.

"Thank you, buddy," she said quietly. She was happy to discover the gun was loaded because she wouldn't have had a clue as to where to look for the ammunition. She made sure the safety was off before making her way down the hall to the bar.

"Get up!" she heard Sharon yell, and she tensed, listening intently for Taylor's voice, but there was no response.

Callie took a deep breath in through her nose and let it out through her mouth before coming around the corner. Sharon was behind the bar, her back to Callie. There was a gun on the bar, not far from where Sharon was standing. She was bending over, obviously trying to pull Taylor to her feet, but Callie couldn't see Taylor from where she was standing. She walked a couple of steps closer to the bar and aimed her gun center mass.

"Police!" she shouted, adrenaline pumping furiously through her body. "Put your hands up!"

Sharon grabbed the gun as she spun around toward her. Callie pulled the trigger without giving Sharon a chance to realize what was happening. Sharon dropped to the floor and the bottle behind her exploded as the bullet ripped through it.

Callie crouched down at the same time, just in case she got back up to take a shot of her own. She froze when she heard Sharon begin laughing.

"You're a fucking cop?" she asked. "Well, isn't that just fan-fucking-tastic. Say good-bye to your little girlfriend."

Callie heard a glass break, and a couple of seconds later, there was a shot from behind the bar. Time seemed to stand still and it felt like her heart had jumped into her throat. She was having trouble breathing. She realized Randy had crouched down next to her, and his arm was around her shoulders.

"It's okay, Callie, reinforcements are here," he said softly.

She then noticed there were about half a dozen cops in the bar. Why hadn't they shown up two minutes earlier? She jumped to her feet and tried to get to Taylor, but Randy stopped her, spinning her around so she was facing him.

"I have to make sure she's all right," Callie said, pulling her arm away from him.

"Callie?" she heard a voice behind her say. The relief washed over her at the sound of Taylor's voice. Randy let her go and she rushed to Taylor's side. She dropped to the floor next to Taylor, holding her head in her lap. "I'm okay, Callie."

"I can't say the same for Sharon," Callie said softly, looking at the woman on the floor a few feet away, a hole in the middle of her forehead. Her eyes were staring at them, but there was no life there. She'd never been so happy to see someone dead in her life. That was when she saw the knife on the floor next to the body and realized what must have happened.

"Back here!" she heard a booming voice say, and then there were cops and paramedics all around her. She got pushed unceremoniously to the side, and Randy pulled her toward the door.

"Give them room to work, okay?" he said, glancing over her shoulder toward the bar. "I heard someone say she hasn't been shot, so she's going to be fine."

"She shot Sharon," Callie said, meeting his eyes. He nodded. "Sharon's dead."

"Clear case of self-defense if you ask me," he said. He guided her outside and to his car, where he got her situated in the passenger seat.

"She had a knife," Callie said, looking back at the doors to the bar. "I think she must have dropped the gun when she went down to get away from my shot. Taylor had to have grabbed it, and when she came at her with the knife, she shot her."

"Like I said," Randy said with a grin. "Self-defense."

"I could have lost her."

"But you didn't. She's going to be fine." They both looked at the doors when the paramedics came out with Taylor on a stretcher. "You should ride with her. I'll call your sister and then meet you at the hospital."

Callie got up without a word, and made her way to the ambulance.

CHAPTER TWENTY-NINE

Callie opened her eyes but couldn't immediately identify where she was. She looked around the room, and the steady beeping coming from her left was enough to tell her she was in the hospital. She tried to sit up, but Quinn was at her side almost instantly.

"Whoa, there," she said as she gently held her down. "Not a good idea."

"What am I doing here?" she asked. "Where's Taylor?"

"You passed out in the ambulance," Quinn said. "When you came down from the adrenaline high, you just crashed. They hooked you up to some fluids and decided to monitor your heart until you came to, just in case."

"Where's Taylor?" she asked again, getting frustrated with Quinn talking about her condition. She needed to know about Taylor. "Is she okay?"

"She can go home in the morning," Quinn said. "No concussion, which I think surprised everyone given the knot on her head. She's got a couple of bruised ribs, and some cuts on her hand from a broken glass. Nothing too serious. She's pretty anxious to see you though."

"Then let me up."

"Just sit still for a minute. I've pushed your call button, and the nurse will be here in a minute. Grace is with Taylor right now."

Callie closed her eyes and she felt tears coming. She turned her face away from Quinn so she wouldn't be able to see. The events of the night rushed back to her, and she couldn't stop the sob that escaped her.

"Hey, Callie?" Quinn placed a hand on her shoulder and squeezed gently. "Everything's okay. You're both safe, and Sharon's gone."

"I thought I was going to lose her, Quinn," Callie said, refusing to look at her. There was a window in her line of sight, but the curtains were closed, so she couldn't see out. It was still a much more acceptable option than having her sister see her break down though.

"But you didn't," Quinn said softly. Callie felt the bed move as Quinn sat beside her. She was surprised when she grabbed her hand and tried to get her to turn so she could see her face. "I'm your sister. We grew up together. Hell, we did almost *everything* together, Callie. I've seen you cry. It isn't anything to be ashamed of."

Callie squeezed the hand that was holding hers and accepted the tissue Quinn offered with her other hand. She wiped her nose and tried to get rid of the tears on her cheeks before finally looking at her.

"You love her, don't you?" Quinn asked. When Callie didn't answer, not because she couldn't, but because she was scared to admit it, Quinn smiled. "I'm pretty sure she feels the same way about you, and I'm so sorry I gave you a hard time about it in the beginning. I see how the two of you look at each other, and I honestly haven't seen her this happy since before Andrea died. I'm happy for both of you."

"Jesus, you'd better get the hell out of here before I start to think you have a heart," Callie said, causing them both to laugh. The nurse walked in then, and Callie gave Quinn a serious look. "Thank you, Quinn. I don't know what I'd do without you, you know that, right?"

Quinn simply nodded before she stood to give the nurse room, and she thought Quinn looked as if she might start crying any second. A thought struck her, and she grabbed Quinn's hand again.

"Taylor's parents are coming tomorrow. Has anyone called them?"

"She called them herself as soon as she was settled in a room for the night."

"What time is it?"

"It's after two in the morning," the nurse said as she fussed with checking Callie out.

"I need to go see her," Callie said.

"Maybe you didn't hear me say it's after two in the morning?" The nurse gave her a look that left no room for argument. Callie wondered if the woman even knew how to smile. "You aren't going anywhere until the doctor comes in at seven."

"Calliope, what the hell are you doing back here?" David asked as he walked in and moved to her side, effectively pushing the nurse out of the way.

"I'm so happy to see you I won't even bitch about you calling me Calliope," she said, the relief almost physical in nature. Less than ten minutes later, she'd given him the whole story, and he was in the process of getting her discharged and making arrangements to have her go to Taylor's room.

"Thank you," she said as she hugged him when he brought them to Taylor's room but stopped right outside of it. "You're the best, Dave."

"Just take care of yourself, all right? I don't want to see you back here anytime soon."

"She broke up with me," she said when David was gone.

"I have faith you two can get past that." Quinn squeezed her shoulder briefly. "You're a Burke. You can convince her you belong together."

Quinn stood there by her side, waiting for her to be ready to walk in. Callie looked at her and opened the door. Grace stood from the chair she was sitting in and came to hug Callie.

"She keeps waking up and asking for you," she said quietly. She took Quinn's hand and led her back to the door. "We'll go get some coffee and be back in a bit."

Callie nodded, feeling like she was going to burst into tears again. She didn't even want to think about what she'd do without either one of them in her life. She finally glanced over to the bed where Taylor was, and was met by a bright smile.

"It's about time you got here," she said. "I was worried sick about you after you passed out in the ambulance."

Callie felt her face flush and she scratched the back of her neck. "Yeah, sorry about that. I guess I just crashed after all the excitement was over."

"Come here," Taylor said, holding a hand out to her. When Callie sat, she brought Taylor's hand to her lips but never broke eye contact.

"I don't know what I would have done if I'd lost you," she said, her voice barely above a whisper as she once again felt tears threatening.

"But you didn't. We're both here, and we're both alive." Taylor squeezed her hand. "I'm just thankful you were there, and Randy knew what I wanted him to do with my phone."

"And to think you were worried about *my* job being high risk." Callie grinned, and Taylor laughed, although it was obviously painful based on the wince she sported. "Who thought yours would be more dangerous than mine?"

"Not so fast there, tiger," she said with a shake of her head, but she looked thoughtful. "I may have taken the butt of a gun to the face, but you actually got shot. I think yours still takes top honors as being the most dangerous. But you're right. Given the right circumstances, I guess any job can be dangerous."

Callie was overcome with emotion. She leaned down, careful not to hurt Taylor's ribs, and placed a soft kiss on her lips.

"I love you," she whispered against her lips before pulling back. Taylor was staring at her and Callie wondered if she'd even heard what she said. She only had a few seconds to speculate on it before Taylor reached up and touched her cheek.

"Callie, I—"

"I know this isn't the ideal place to make such a declaration, and I really don't expect you to say it in return, okay?" Callie knew the words might not be received well, but the look of fear she saw on Taylor's face made her seriously rethink sharing it. Oh, well. Too late now. "I'm just a little emotionally overwhelmed at the moment, and I needed to say it. I needed to let you know how I felt. But no pressure, I promise."

Callie felt the tightness in her chest ease a bit when Taylor smiled and nodded. And she felt better about sharing as she watched Taylor wipe her eyes.

"You called your parents kind of late, huh?" Callie asked, deciding a change of subject was warranted.

"I was going to wait until morning, but Quinn and Grace wouldn't let me." She smiled.

"They're still coming though, right?"

"I wouldn't be surprised if they were already on their way," Taylor said, attempting again to laugh, but she winced and pressed a hand to her side.

"Good, because you probably shouldn't be alone for the first couple of days at least. Especially with a dog that might jump on you in his puppy like exuberance." Callie looked away when Taylor gave her another strange look. "I mean, I just wouldn't want anything to happen to you. Blaze can get a little rough when he's excited."

"Callie, look at me," she said. Callie didn't do as she'd requested right away, so she squeezed her hand. "Don't make me hurt you, because I'm pretty sure it would hurt me too, but I will if I have to." Callie met her eyes then and Taylor gave her a slow smile. "I assumed you would want to stay with me. If you don't, that's fine."

"I wasn't sure you'd want me to." She winked at her and smiled back. "I can get a little rough when I'm excited too, you know."

"I know this about you, but I think I can handle it. Will you stay with me, at least for a few days?"

"Of course I will. I can sleep on the couch. Because, you know, you ended things between us."

"I'd like to revisit that, if you want to. I told my parents we're more than friends." Taylor grinned when Callie pretended to be shocked. "The couch is a sleeper, and my parents can sleep on it. You're more than welcome to sleep in my bed with me."

"I would love to revisit that, Ms. Fletcher. But I have a bone to pick. I slept on that uncomfortable couch for two nights, and you never thought to tell me it pulled out into a bed?"

"Forgive me?" Taylor smiled at her, and Callie felt her insides turn to mush.

She leaned down and kissed her, fully intending it to be quick and chaste, but Taylor evidently had other ideas. She put a hand on the back of Callie's neck and pulled her closer as she deepened the kiss.

Callie wasn't going to argue.

CHAPTER THIRTY

Taylor woke the next morning before the sun came up and was surprised to find Callie in a chair next to the hospital bed, her head against Taylor's hip and a hand resting on her stomach. Taylor put a hand over hers and smiled, remembering their conversation from the night before.

She said she loved me.

She had to admit, when Callie said those words, it had surprised her, but not in a bad way. Taylor hadn't known what to say in response, and frankly, she wasn't sure she'd have been able to say anything, even if she had known what to say.

Do I love her?

Until Sharon hit her with the gun, it wasn't something she'd given any real thought to since her mother mentioned it on Christmas Eve. She still loved Andrea. She knew she probably always would, and she was pretty sure Callie knew it too. But could Grace have been right? Was it possible to find that kind of love twice in a lifetime? Taylor always believed she and Andrea would grow old together, but then she was taken far too soon.

When Quinn had been questioning whether or not it would be wise to gamble losing her friendship with Grace by declaring her love a few months ago, Taylor gave her some advice that had made perfect sense at the time. She'd told her she needed to decide if trying to make a life with Grace was worth the risk. And for her, loving Andrea had been worth the risk. Even with everything that happened, she wouldn't have given up any of it just to be spared the loss. Maybe it was time she took her own advice, or at least seriously considered it.

Would loving Callie be worth the risk to her? She began to absently run her fingers through Callie's hair as she considered the question. She was funny, caring, and extremely charming. Blaze was obviously enamored with her. She'd been Andrea's best friend, so apparently Andrea had seen the good in her.

And Callie had been the first one to take the risk by declaring her love for Taylor, which wasn't something she could simply dismiss. She sighed and closed her eyes, wishing Andrea could give her some sign. She chuckled at her foolishness and glanced at Callie, who was still asleep.

"I will always love you, Andrea," she whispered, looking at the ceiling. "But I think it might really be time to move on. I hope you'll understand."

Callie stirred then, and Taylor removed her hand from her hair. When Callie raised her head and looked at her, Taylor didn't fight the feeling that came over her. Callie *was* worth the risk. She smiled, but saying the words here, in the hospital room, didn't seem right. She'd wait until later to tell her how she felt.

"What's going on here?" Taylor asked when she and Callie arrived at her house. She looked warily at Quinn's car parked in her driveway. When they walked inside, there was the most wonderful aroma coming from the kitchen.

Her parents had arrived at the hospital before Taylor was discharged, so she'd given them her keys in order for them to get settled and to allow Blaze back into his house. Apparently, they'd let Quinn and Grace in as well.

"They wanted to help out," her mother said with a smile when she met them just inside the front door. She had Blaze on a leash, which Taylor knew from experience he wasn't liking much, but he sat there looking at her, his tail wagging. It was obvious he knew something was wrong with her. "They're making lunch for us."

"Welcome home," Linda Burke said when she walked out of the kitchen and found them all huddled just inside the door. She took everyone's coats and ushered them into the kitchen. Taylor felt as though she'd been gone for weeks, when in reality, she'd been here less than twenty-four hours ago. "How are you feeling?"

"A little sore here," she answered, indicating her ribs. She touched her head where there was a rather large bruise, and more than a few stitches. "And I have a bit of a headache."

"You want one of the painkillers they gave you at the hospital?" Callie asked, pulling the bottle out of her pocket. Taylor nodded and watched her go to the sink to get her a glass of water.

"You look much better than you did last night," Quinn said.

"But still a mess, right?" Taylor asked good-naturedly.

"You said it, I didn't." Quinn grinned and turned back to what she was cooking.

"You're going to have to take care of the bar for a few days," Callie told Quinn as she squeezed by her on her way back to Taylor. "The doctor said she should take it easy for a while."

"Yeah, about that." Quinn handed the spatula to Grace and kissed her cheek before coming and sitting at the table with Taylor. "You still want me to become your general manager?"

"Are you serious?" Taylor thought she must be dreaming. It was something she'd been trying to get Quinn to do for months, but she'd always refused. Taylor watched her for a moment, then looked at Callie, who was smiling. "Don't joke about this, Quinn."

"No joke," Quinn assured her. "Grace and I talked it over, and we decided now that you have a life outside the bar again, you shouldn't feel like you need to be there all the time."

"I think I should be offended by that, but I'll let it slide for now," Taylor said. "You have a life outside the bar too, you know."

"Yeah, but you know," Quinn said before leaning close to her and whispering, "you're old."

Taylor backhanded her in the stomach and laughed. "I'm two months older than you, you bitch." She glared at Callie. "Did you have anything to do with this?"

"They told me this morning," Callie said, her hands in the air. "I had no idea."

"Honey," her mother said from where she was standing behind Taylor. "Maybe you should take her up on it. You'd be able to do things you always wanted to do."

Of course she was going to take her up on it, but she had no intention of letting Quinn know it yet. It might be nice to let her sweat about it for a while. It would serve her right for having turned her down on the offer for so long.

"I'll think about it," she said, but Quinn's smirk let her know she wasn't fooling her.

"Okay, we have homemade chicken soup, thanks to Linda," Grace said with an affectionate smile for Callie and Quinn's mother. "And Quinn made some pretty awesome grilled cheese sandwiches, if I do say so myself."

"I'll get yours," Callie said, leaning down to speak into Taylor's ear. She planted a kiss on her cheek before walking over to the stove to get their soup.

"I'm so happy you finally decided to let someone in, honey," her mother said as they both watched Callie and Quinn playfully shoving each other. Taylor felt her father place a hand on her shoulder and squeeze gently.

"We both are," he said. "And I like her. It's pretty obvious she cares a great deal for you."

"She told me she loves me," Taylor said, not having intended to say it out loud, but there it was. Her heart fluttered when Callie turned and winked at her. She was even more sure now than she had been that morning of what she felt for Callie. And she couldn't explain why, but she had the feeling that Andrea approved.

"Are you okay?" Callie asked when they both went out into the backyard with Blaze a little later. Everyone else was in the living room, talking about plans for the evening, of which nobody seemed to have other than watching the festivities on television.

"I'm fine," Taylor said with a smile.

Callie stood there watching Blaze run around the yard, apparently looking for the perfect spot to pee. She worried about Taylor. She'd shot someone. Not only that, but she'd killed someone. Killing someone would mess with anybody's head, wouldn't it?

"Hey," Taylor said, putting an arm around her waist and pulling her closer. "What's on your mind?"

"Maybe you should talk to someone," she said gently. "A professional."

"For what?"

"Taylor, you killed someone. If that happened to me, I'd have to spend weeks with a department psychiatrist to make sure I was able to process it properly."

"She was going to kill me," Taylor said. "She said as much after you shot at her. And she said after she took care of me, she was going to kill you. There was no way I was going to let that happen to you. It was self-defense, Callie. I don't regret what I did."

"Promise me something." Callie waited for her to nod her agreement. "If you ever do start to have problems because of what happened, promise me you'll see someone."

"I promise," she said before pulling her even closer and kissing her. "But right now, I just feel relief to know she won't ever be able to bother either one of us again."

"Is this a private party, or can anyone join?" Quinn asked when she walked out to join them. "Damn, it's cold out here."

"That's why we're wearing jackets, you idiot," Callie said with a laugh.

"Come back inside. We're getting ready to leave."

They followed her in, and Grace made sure to tell her what to do with the roast she'd been cooking all day in the slow cooker.

"It's your mother's recipe," she said to Callie. "Your favorite, right?"

"Everything my mother cooks is my favorite," Callie answered with a quick kiss to her mother's cheek. "Especially when she cooks it just for me."

"Don't fool yourself, Callie," her mother said before giving Taylor a hug. "I made this one for Taylor, not you."

"Even better." Callie grinned and slipped her arm around Taylor's waist.

❖

Nobody seemed to be able to make it until the ball dropped in Times Square at midnight. Taylor's parents both kept dozing off, and Taylor had gone up to bed at about twenty after eleven. There was only fifteen minutes left to wait, but Callie said her good nights and headed down the hall to Callie's bedroom. She hesitated for a moment before opening the door and walking in.

She smiled when her eyes met Taylor's, who was sitting up in bed reading a book. She had the sheet pulled up over her chest, but Callie was pretty sure she wasn't wearing any clothes. Callie went to sit next to her on the edge of the bed and leaned over to kiss her.

"You couldn't make it either?" Taylor asked.

"I decided to have mercy on your parents," Callie answered. She lifted the sheet and peeked under, smiling to find out she was right. "You're naked."

"You're not."

"That's easily remedied." Callie stood and pulled her shirt over her head. She stopped as she was about to let it fall to the floor when she looked at the bedside table for the first time. It was empty except for the lamp. She looked at Taylor. "What happened to the picture of you and Andrea?"

Taylor glanced over to where the framed photo had been and shrugged.

"Come here," she said, patting the edge of the bed. Callie sat and allowed Taylor to take her hand. "It's going on four years, Callie. It's time to move on, don't you think?"

"You don't have to put the pictures of her away though."

"I haven't, at least not yet, but I will eventually." Taylor smiled and brushed Callie's cheek with the backs of her fingers. "She will always be in my heart. I hope you know that."

"Of course I do."

"She was my once in a lifetime love."

Callie tensed, feeling as if there might be a brush off on the horizon. She looked away and started to stand, but Taylor stopped her with a hand on her arm.

"But I'm willing to find out if it's possible to have that kind of love twice in a lifetime," Taylor said, and it took Callie a moment to realize what she was saying. She took Callie's hand and entwined their fingers. "I love you, Callie, and I want to find out if that kind of love is possible with you."

"You do?" Callie smiled.

"I do," Taylor said with a nod. "I think you should finish getting undressed and join me in bed now. But we're only going to sleep, okay? My ribs are still sore."

She didn't need to be told twice. She stripped and crawled under the covers, holding Taylor gently in her arms so as not to cause any further pain. She sighed with contentment and realized she was happier in that moment than she'd ever been in her life.

"I love you, baby," she whispered into Taylor's ear.

"I love you, too," Taylor replied before turning her head to kiss her. "Now get some sleep. We have a lot of living to do, and I can't think of a more perfect time to start than the first day of a new year."

About the Author

PJ Trebelhorn was born and raised in the greater metropolitan area of Portland, Oregon. Her love of sports—mainly baseball and ice hockey—was fueled in part by her father's interests. She likes to brag about the fact that her uncle managed the Milwaukee Brewers for five years, and the Chicago Cubs for one year.

PJ now resides in western New York with her wife, Cheryl; their three cats; and one very neurotic dog. When not writing or reading, PJ enjoys watching movies, playing on the Playstation, and spending way too much time with stupid games on Facebook. She still roots for the Flyers, Phillies, and Eagles, even though she's now in Sabres and Bills territory.

Books Available from Bold Strokes Books

A Heart to Call Home by Jeannie Levig. When Jessie Weldon returns to her hometown after thirty years, can she and her childhood crush Dakota Scott heal the tragic past that links them? (978-1-63555-059-7)

Children of the Healer by Barbara Ann Wright. Life becomes desperate for ex-soldier Cordelia Ross when the indigenous aliens of her planet are drawn into a civil war and old enemies linger in the shadows. Book Three of the Godfall Series. (978-1-63555-031-3)

Hearts Like Hers by Melissa Brayden. Coffee shop owner Autumn Primm is ready to cut loose and live a little, but is the baggage that comes with out-of-towner Kate Carpenter too heavy for anything long term? (978-1-63555-014-6)

Love at Cooper's Creek by Missouri Vaun. Shaw Daily flees corporate life to find solace in the rural Blue Ridge Mountains, but escapism eludes her when her attentions are captured by small town beauty Kate Elkins. (978-1-62639-960-0)

Somewhere Over Lorain Road by Bud Gundy. Over forty years after murder allegations shattered the Esker family, can Don Esker find the true killer and clear his dying father's name? (978-1-63555-124-2)

Twice in a Lifetime by PJ Trebelhorn. Detective Callie Burke can't deny the growing attraction to her late friend's widow, Taylor Fletcher, who also happens to own the bar where Callie's sister works. (978-1-63555-033-7)

Undiscovered Affinity by Jane Hardee. Will a no strings attached affair be enough to break Olivia's control and convince Cardic that love does exist? (978-1-63555-061-0)

Between Sand and Stardust by Tina Michele. Are the lifelong bonds of love strong enough to conquer time, distance, and heartache when Haven Thorne and Willa Bennette are given another chance at forever? (978-1-62639-940-2)

Charming the Vicar by Jenny Frame. When magician and atheist Finn Kane seeks refuge in an English village after a spiritual crisis, can local vicar Bridget Claremont restore her faith in life and love? (978-1-63555-029-0)

Data Capture by Jesse J. Thoma. Lola Walker is undercover on the hunt for cybercriminals while trying not to notice the woman who might be perfectly wrong for her for all the right reasons. (978-1-62639-985-3)

Epicurean Delights by Renee Roman. Ariana Marks had no idea a leisure swim would lead to being rescued, in more ways than one, by the charismatic Hudson Frost. (978-1-63555-100-6)

Heart of the Devil by Ali Vali. We know most of Cain and Emma Casey's story, but *Heart of the Devil* will take you back to where it began one fateful night with a tray loaded with beer. (978-1-63555-045-0)

Known Threat by Kara A. McLeod. When Special Agent Ryan O'Connor reluctantly questions who protects the Secret Service, she learns courage truly is found in unlikely places. Agent O'Connor Series #3. (978-1-63555-132-7)

Seer and the Shield by D. Jackson Leigh. Time is running out for the Dragon Horse Army while two unlikely heroines struggle to put aside their attraction and find a way to stop a deadly cult. Dragon Horse War, Book 3. (978-1-63555-170-9)

Sinister Justice by Steve Pickens. When a vigilante targets citizens of Jake Finnigan's hometown, Jake and his partner Sam fall under suspicion themselves as they investigate the murders. (978-1-63555-094-8)

The Universe Between Us by Jane C. Esther. Ana Mitchell must make the hardest choice of her life: the promise of new love Jolie Dann on Earth, or a humanity-saving mission to colonize Mars. (978-1-63555-106-8)

Touch by Kris Bryant. Can one touch heal a heart? (978-1-63555-084-9)

Change in Time by Robyn Nyx. Working in the past is hell on your future. The Extractor Series: Book Two. (978-1-62639-880-1)

Love After Hours by Radclyffe. When Gina Antonelli agrees to renovate Carrie Longmire's new house, she doesn't welcome Carrie's overtures at friendship or her own unexpected attraction. A Rivers Community Novel. (978-1-63555-090-0)

Nantucket Rose by CF Frizzell. Maggie Jordan can't wait to convert an historic Nantucket home into a B&B, but doesn't expect to fall for mariner Ellis Chilton, who has more claim to the house than Maggie realizes. (978-1-63555-056-6)

Picture Perfect by Lisa Moreau. Falling in love wasn't supposed to be part of the stakes for Olive and Gabby, rival photographers in the competition of a lifetime. (978-1-62639-975-4)

Set the Stage by Karis Walsh. Actress Emilie Danvers takes the stage again in Ashland, Oregon, little realizing that landscaper Arden Philips is about to offer her a very personal romantic lead role. (978-1-63555-087-0)

Strike a Match by Fiona Riley. When their attempts at matchmaking fizzle out, firefighter Sasha and reluctant millionairess Abby find themselves turning to each other to strike a perfect match. (978-1-62639-999-0)

The Price of Cash by Ashley Bartlett. Cash Braddock is doing her best to keep her business afloat, stay out of jail, and avoid Detective Kallen. It's not working. (978-1-62639-708-8)

Under Her Wing by Ronica Black. At Angel's Wings Rescue, dogs are usually the ones saved, but when quiet Kassandra Haden meets outspoken owner Jayden Beaumont, the two stubborn women just might end up saving each other. (978-1-63555-077-1)

Underwater Vibes by Mickey Brent. When Hélène, a translator in Brussels, Belgium, meets Sylvie, a young Greek photographer and swim coach, unsettling feelings hijack Hélène's mind and body—even her poems. (978-1-63555-002-3)

A More Perfect Union by Carsen Taite. Major Zoey Granger and DC fixer Rook Daniels risk their reputations for a chance at true love while dealing with a scandal that threatens to rock the military. (978-1-62639-754-5)

Arrival by Gun Brooke. The spaceship *Pathfinder* reaches its passengers' new homeworld where danger lurks in the shadows while Pamas Seclan disembarks and finds unexpected love in young science genius Darmiya Do Voy. (978-1-62639-859-7)

Captain's Choice by VK Powell. Architect Kerstin Anthony's life is going to plan until Bennett Carlyle, the first girl she ever kissed, is assigned to her latest and most important project, a police district substation. (978-1-62639-997-6)

Falling Into Her by Erin Zak. Pam Phillips, widow at the age of forty, meets Kathryn Hawthorne, local Chicago celebrity, and it changes her life forever—in ways she hadn't even considered possible. (978-1-63555-092-4)

Hookin' Up by MJ Williamz. Will Leah get what she needs from casual hookups or will she see the love she desires right in front of her? (978-1-63555-051-1)

King of Thieves by Shea Godfrey. When art thief Casey Marinos meets bounty hunter Finnegan Starkweather, the crimes of the past just might set the stage for a payoff worth more than she ever dreamed possible. (978-1-63555-007-8)

Lucy's Chance by Jackie D. As a serial killer haunts the streets, Lucy tries to stitch up old wounds with her first love in the wake of a small town's rapid descent into chaos. (978-1-63555-027-6)

Right Here, Right Now by Georgia Beers. When Alicia Wright moves into the office next door to Lacey Chamberlain's accounting firm, Lacey is about to find out that sometimes the last person you want is exactly the person you need. (978-1-63555-154-9)

Strictly Need to Know by MB Austin. Covert operator Maji Rios will do whatever she must to complete her mission, but saving a gorgeous stranger from Russian mobsters was not in her plans. (978-1-63555-114-3)

Tailor-Made by Yolanda Wallace. Tailor Grace Henderson doesn't date clients, but when she meets gender-bending model Dakota Lane, she's tempted to throw all the rules out the window. (978-1-63555-081-8)

Time Will Tell by M. Ullrich. With the ability to time travel, Eva Caldwell will have to decide between having it all and erasing it all. (978-1-63555-088-7)

A Date to Die by Anne Laughlin. Someone is killing people close to Detective Kay Adler, who must look to her own troubled past for a suspect. There she finds more than one person seeking revenge against her. (978-1-63555-023-8)

Captured Soul by Laydin Michaels. Can Kadence Munroe save the woman she loves from a twisted killer, or will she lose her to a collector of souls? (978-1-62639-915-0)

Dawn's New Day by TJ Thomas. Can Dawn Oliver and Cam Cooper, two women who have loved and lost, open their hearts to love again? (978-1-63555-072-6)

Definite Possibility by Maggie Cummings. Sam Miller is just out for good times, but Lucy Weston makes her realize happily ever after is a definite possibility. (978-1-62639-909-9)

Eyes Like Those by Melissa Brayden. Isabel Chase and Taylor Andrews struggle between love and ambition from the writers' room on one of Hollywood's hottest TV shows. (978-1-63555-012-2)

Heart's Orders by Jaycie Morrison. Helen Tucker and Tee Owens escape hardscrabble lives to careers in the Women's Army Corps, but more than their hearts are at risk as friendship blossoms into love. (978-1-63555-073-3)

Hiding Out by Kay Bigelow. Treat Dandridge is unaware that her life is in danger from the murderer who is hunting the woman she's falling in love with, Mickey Heiden. (978-1-62639-983-9)

Omnipotence Enough by Sophia Kell Hagin. Can the tiny tool that abducted war veteran Jamie Gwynmorgan accidentally acquires help her escape an unknown enemy to reclaim her stolen life and the woman she deeply loves? (978-1-63555-037-5)

Summer's Cove by Aurora Rey. Emerson Lange moved to Provincetown to live in the moment, but when she meets Darcy Belo and her son Liam, her quest for summer romance becomes a family affair. (978-1-62639-971-6)

The Road to Wings by Julie Tizard. Lieutenant Casey Tompkins, Air Force student pilot, has to fly with the toughest instructor, Captain Kathryn "Hard Ass" Hardesty, fly a supersonic jet, and deal with a growing forbidden attraction. (978-1-62639-988-4)